Eddy Shade
and the UnSeelie Court

Eddy Shade
and the UnSeelie Court

Steffan Becker

Library of Congress Control Number: 2013918547
ISBN: Hardcover   978-1-4931-1417-7
                Softcover   978-1-4931-1416-0
                Ebook   978-1-4931-1418-4

Rev. date: 10/21/2013

To order additional copies of this book, contact:
Xlibris LLC
1-888-795-4274
www.Xlibris.com
Orders@Xlibris.com
132786

Contents

Eddy Shade and The City in the Lake

I dedicate this book to my wife and kids.
With out there support, input and helpfully suggestions,
this story would not have been possible.

Chapter 1

Raid

Eddy and Carl were sitting in a dark blue station wagon outside of a small office building in downtown Denver. Eddy stared out his window and yawned as one of the street lights turned off, making the already dark winter night even darker. It was an over cast night, not that it would have mattered much. It was a new moon, leaving it so the only light they had was the scattered street lights that could not decide if they should be on or not, and then there was the dim yellow light above the door to the office building they had parked across the street from in order to watch.

Carl had insisted they use his car for the stake out. Carl claimed it was because it was roomier, but Eddy knew that what he really meant was that he would not easily fit into Eddy's four door sedan. Carl stood seven feet tall and was built like a pro wrestler, well a pro wrestler with a slight bit of a gut. Eddy didn't know if Carl's appearance was typical for a giant, Carl being the only one Eddy had ever met, and was not certain if it would be polite to ask, or even how to work it into a conversation.

Carl took a drink of what had long sense become a very cold cup of coffee and looked back out the window. "You know Eddy, I am glad that your friend Xander zapped your brain over the summer, and that you found out about the magical world. Gives me someone to bring along on stakeouts and all that. There is not a lot of a CDMA presence in the Denver Police Department, let alone at our station. Surprising really, given Denver's large magical population."

The CDMA was the Colorado Department of Magical Affairs. It was kind of a secret police buried inside of the police department that specialized in dealing with Colorado's non human criminals. Eddy had found out about all of it earlier in the year after he had witnessed a man struck by lightning under a bridge over the summer. The department had dismissed it as nothing more then a random lighting strike. Eddy however was not convinced and had persuade the case on his own. He had decide to tell his best friend Xander about it, who in turn had sent a charge through Eddy's brain, allowing him to access a closed off portion of the human brain that allowed him to see through what was referred to as the veil. The veil being a magical barrier that allows magical creatures to freely walk among us while looking just like every one else, shielding humanity from their true identities.

"I guess I know now why you were often so closed lipped about your cases" Eddy said.

"Yeah, sorry about that, but we try and keep the human world from knowing about us. It's better that way. Can you imagine what kind of pandemonium would ensue if people found out that their neighbor was a creatures that child hood stories say would eat them. Legends and fairy tails have not been kind. According to them I should be grinding your bones into flour right now. I mean seriously, who came up with that any ways?"

Eddy just smiled. He had learned that the subject of myth and legend could be a touchy subject for a lot of the magical population, some more then others. Carl especially hated stories about giants. They nearly always made them into the villain, and here Carl was, a cop, working to protect the very people who grew up believing that his kind were monsters.

"Their here" Carl said as he leaned forward to try and get a better look at the front of the building.

Eddy looked as well and saw seven people slip in through the door of the building. Carl had not told him what the species was they were tailing, but Eddy had a pretty good guess that they were not human. The fact that there were seven of them worried Eddy more then just a little bit. He knew from an encounter over the summer that wraiths were known to travel in groups of seven, and he was in no mood to deal with wraiths tonight, or any other night to be perfectly honest.

Eddy heard the pop of a car door opening and looked over to see Carl getting out of the car. "Where are you going?" Eddy asked.

"I'm going in" was all Carl said before he closed his car door and quickly began walking towards the front of the old gray one story office building. Eddy scrambled out of the car and had to practically run to catch up with Carl. There was no denying the large man could cover a lot of ground quickly.

"Carl slow down" Eddy whispered loudly. He quickly looked both ways as he crossed the street. He paused as he looked towards the far end of the building. Standing in the gap between it and the neighboring building he saw a figure standing in the shadows. From what Eddy could see it appeared to be a tall woman with long silver hair, and a sleek dress that bellowed out at the bottom "Carl hold up."

Carl finally stopped and looked back at Eddy "what is it?"

"There is a woman over there" he whispered as he pointed towards the far end of the building.

"Over where?" Carl whispered in a loud hiss as he turned around to look at Eddy.

Suddenly a strong gust of wind came up. As the wind blew down the street it picked up the gravel and sand the city had put down on the roads to help prevent cars from sliding on the ice during the last snow storm and carried it down the road towards them. The gravel pelted the men in the face, and they had to look away in order to avoid the sharp sting of it hitting them and burning their eyes. When Eddy looked back towards the end of the building the woman was gone.

"She's gone" Eddy whispered.

"Then we better hurry. If she is with them then they may already be on to us" Carl said. The two men reached the building and pressed themselves against the outside wall on opposite sides of the door. "Did you bring your sword?" Carl asked Eddy as he pulled a small hammer shaped key chain out of his pocket. Eddy nodded and pulled a small antique butter knife out of his jacket pocket and held it up. "Good" Carl said with a nod of his own. Carl held the arm that was holding the key chain out to the side and the small hammer expanded into a large sledge hammer with a broad brass head. Eddy held his arm out as well, and the little knife shimmered before it expanded into a large silver sword.

Carl smiled at Eddy, then stepped away from the wall, drew back the hammer and slammed its broad head full force into the door. The door splintered and buckled as it collapsed inwards on itself. Carl rushed into the hall that sat behind the now missing door with Eddy close at his heals behind him. They quickly came to another door at the end of the short hall they had entered, and Carl promptly kicked it in with out ever taking a break in his momentum.

There was then a loud slurry of shouts and commotion as people in the room began to scramble around, nearly tripping over each other in an attempt to make their way out through another door in the back of the room. There were only five people in the room, and much to Eddy's relief not a one of them was a wraith. Most had blond hair, pale skin and pointed ears. One, who was shorter then the others, had black hair and eyebrows that looked almost like some one had glued large quantities of fluffy down feathers to his head.

"Halt in the name of the law. This is the Denver Police, we are acting under CDMA clearance. I said HALT!" Carl seemed to puff up slightly, clearly getting frustrated. "Eyes" he yelled and Eddy shut his eyes tightly, barely getting them closed in time. Even with his eyes closed he could still see the bright flash of light that had originated from Carl. It was quickly fallowed by a small short sizzling sound. When Eddy opened his eyes he saw that all the men were laying on the floor with their hands held tight over their eyes, as they laid there curled up into a fetal position, their skin reddened like they had been sunburned.

"We are missing two" Eddy pointed out.

"Possibly more. We don't know if there was already some one in here before they came in. Then there is your mystery woman you saw outside. We don't know if she is involved with this or not." Carl nodded towards the door in the back of the room "come on" he said as he began to walk towards it.

When they opened the door in the back of the room the long hall behind it was completely black with not even a glow from emergency lights to illuminate it. They peered into the darkness to see if they could see any one lurking inside, when suddenly there came a low growling sound. The low growl grew louder, and then slowly a yellow circle the size of a pool ball drifted into the hall, followed soon after by another. The two bright yellow balls floated just shy of three feet off the ground. The two yellow balls began to steadily move towards the two men as the growling began to intensify. Carl held up his free hand and it began to glow, illuminating the hallway. Once the light grew bright enough to reach the two orbs, it became apparent that it was in fact a set of glowing pupil less eyes that belonged to a large pony sized shaggy black dog. The creature snarled, it then leaped suddenly down the hall and through the door, teeth bared as it slammed full force into Eddy.

The large dog hit him hard, causing him to drop his sword as he slammed into the ground. He tried to force the massive head back as he tried frantically to hold the snapping jaws away from his face with one hand, while trying to grab hold of his gun with the other. But he kept being forced to pull his hand back in front of him in order to push the beast back as it kept exerting more and more pressure on him. Suddenly the light in the room dimmed and the enormous dogs body lurched to the side with a tremendous force. Eddy still laying on the floor looked over at the dog as it lay whining on the floor near by. He then looked back the other direction to see Carl holding the large hammer in both hands like it was an enormous golf club.

Eddy took another look back over at the large dog as it limped away whimpering. "What is that thing?" he breathed as he retrieved his sword from where it had landed near by and got back up off the floor.

"Black dog" Carl said as he relight the light in his hand and slowly began to work his large frame through the narrow hall door.

"That is no ordinary black dog" Eddy said as he glanced back before he fallowed Carl into the hall.

"No. Not a black dog as in a dog with black fur. A black dog as in the species. Often used as magical guard dogs. They can see in complete darkness, and are extremely protective, and if they have one here then they are definitely trying to protect something. Tread, lightly."

Carl held out his glowing hand in front of him at eye level as they made their way through the dark hallway. As they made their way forward they would peer into the offices that lined the walls as they passed them, all seeming equally empty of every thing but cobwebs. As they approached a set of aligning doors they began to hear a series of knocking sounds. The sounds seemed to echo as they passed out of the doorway on the right and reverberated down the hallway.

Eddy began to make his way to the door, but Carl put a hand on his shoulder to stop him. He looked over at Carl who in turn made a nodding motion towards the door on the other side of the hall. The two men pressed themselves against the wall as Carl held up a hand with three fingers extended and began counting down by lowering them one by one. When he lowered the final finger the duo rushed through the doorway and into the room.

"Everybody freeze" Carl yelled into the crate filled room. Eddy nervously looked around the room unable to see anyone amongst the closely stacked boxes. Suddenly a short man with bushy feather like eyebrows sprang from behind a filing cabinet and latched onto Carl. Another jumped out of a near by trashcan, knocking it over in the process, and began running towards Eddy.

"Leave the human! Help me subdue the giant" yelled the one holding onto Carl. The one that had jumped out of the trashcan quickly changed directions and climbed up Carl like a monkey climbing a tree. It grabbed hold of the large mans ears, leaned back and then quickly opened its mouth resulting in a loud echoing sound like rock bouncing hard off a cave wall.

Carl fell to his knees and buckled over in pain as the little man continued to rapidly make the loud knocking sound into his ear. Each time the sound would increase in volume, to the point where it began to sound more and more like the sound of gunshots. Carl was trying to reach for his now bleeding ears, but the small man on his arm kept getting in the way. As Carl crouched on the floor Eddy decided to take advantage of the larger man's lowered height, and kicked the small man attached to him in the side of the head causing him to let go of Carl and roll across the floor. He then grabbed a hold of the bushy hair of the man on the giants arm, pulled him backwards, and slammed the hilt of his sword into the little man's bulbous nose.

Carl regained his composure and stood up. He wiped the blood away from his ears as he looked down at the two men on the floor, one unconscious, the other rocking back and forth while he clutched his broken nose. Carl produced a pair of iron shackles and put them on the wrists of the man with the profusely bleeding nose.

"Looks like we found what the dog was guarding" Carl said as he glanced around the room at the crates.

"What are those two?" Eddy asked as he looked at the two men.

"They're called knockers. Normally live under ground, good at finding things, and I think this one is going to tell us what they found and put in the crates."

"Nothing" the knocker spat. "There is nothing but garbage here. You are to late. Nothing but garbage now" and the little man began to laugh.

Chapter 2

Snow

Carl and Eddy were sitting in the back of a non descriptive white delivery truck. The five blue eyed blonds with the pointed ears, of which Carl had informed Eddy were elves, and the three knockers all sat with them. The seven prisoners all had their hands chained together in iron shackles similar to what you would expected to see in some medieval dungeon. Their feet were also shackled, and held securely to the floor at the base of the long benches that lined the sides of the truck. The iron shackles not only served to hold the men in place, but it also hampered any chance of them using even the simplest of magic.

The two men sat in silence for a while, staring at their captives before Carl finally spoke. "So any one here want to tell me what the deal with all the creates we found in there is?" Carl sat quietly for a moment as he leaned forward on his knees and looked across each of the faces that shared the back of the truck with him. "No one?" he finally said. "We already know you are shipping stolen artifacts into the city, most of which come from over seas. All I want you to do is tell me why. What kind of game are we playing here? The more you tell me, the easier things are going to go for you."

"Not if the blue lady finds out it won't" responded one of the knockers.

"And who is the blue lady?" Eddy asked as he leaned forward to better see the small furry man.

"Don't tell them anything" spat the elf that was farthest down the truck. "You know what will happen if we talk." The tall man leaned back and lightly bumped the back of his head on the inside wall of the truck with frustration.

"I know that" the knocker that had spoken shot back. "I am not that stupid. At least she got what she wanted. So we shouldn't end up like Travis."

The elf at the end stood up quickly and tried to lurch towards the knocker, but was held in place by his chains. "Will you just stop talking before you drag us all down with you! I am in no mood to die today do to some ridicules subterranean gnome!"

Carl stood up and pointed a meaty finger at the irate elf "you, just sit right back down" he ordered in a stern voice. The elf complied, and sat back down on the bench with a heavy thump, still giving the smaller man a venomous look. Carl walked over and unlocked the knocker's chains from the wall "Eddy come with me. This one is riding in my car." Eddy got up and fallowed the two men out of the back of the truck making certain to pull down the large sliding door behind him.

Carl had to crouch over as he led the much shorter man over to his over sized station wagon. As Eddy fallowed he wrapped his coat more closely around himself in order to stay warm. The night was quickly getting cold, much colder then Eddy would have expected from mid December in Denver. *It shouldn't be this cold until after the new year* he thought. As Eddy watched Carl load the man into the car he began to notice white specks on the shoulders of the large mans black coat.

"Snow?" Eddy said quietly in disbelief. "It's not supposed to be snowing." He went and stood next to Carl "did you hear anything about snow tonight?" he said as he stared up into the sky at the falling flakes.

Carl looked up at the falling snow as well and scrunched his brow "No I didn't, but it's picking up, and fast."

The snow was falling quite heavily now, seeming to gain momentum with every second, leaving the roads solidly wet and was beginning to pile up in the cooler shadowy parts of the streets. Eddy suddenly began looking around confused as he started to hear a faint crackling noise, similar to the crinkling of tissue paper. "What is that noise?" he asked as he looked over at Carl who was now staring intensely at a near by ally across the street.

"Quiet" Carl said as he listened to the sound. "It almost sounds like someone walking through the snow" he finally whispered.

"But there is not enough snow for it to make that much noise" Eddy pointed out.

"I know that" Carl said with a hint of concern in his voice. His eyes suddenly grew wider "the sound is speeding up" he announced with urgency.

The sidewalk in front of the narrow ally Carl had been staring at, began to turn white, but not from the accumulating snow but from the frost that was rapidly forming in the water on the side walk in front of it. A layer of ice began to form, and then suddenly the ice was pulled back into the dark ally like someone quickly pulling a table cloth off of a table. The light from the dim street lights gleamed off of something in the darkness, and then a gleaming tentacle slithered out of the ally and ran across the street in front of it, moving like a gigantic snake on the hunt. The tentacle was massive, measuring bigger around then a grown mans body, and was completely clear. Another slithering arm of what ever was in the ally crept out along the wall of the building, and was fallowed shortly after by another one on the opposite wall.

Carl and Eddy stared as the large spectral looking arms increased in numbers as the alleys inhabitant made its way to the street. "Guards we need backup out here" Carl called, and the two men that had been in the front of the truck jumped out onto the street. They ran over to stand next to Carl and Eddy. Carl and Eddy drew their guns as did a gray skinned guard with purple eyes. The three men pointed their guns at the center of the slithering mass of clear tentacles as they waited impatiently for the main body to emerge, and finally give them something to shoot at. The second guard, a pale skinned man with a row of stubby horns running across his forehead and glowing yellow eyes, held his hand off to the side. His fingers curled rigidly into the shape of a claw, as a crackling ball of purple electricity formed into its center, and he slowly drew his arm back, like a pitcher ready to throw a fast ball.

Finally a clear mass formed in the center of the ally and slowly made its way out from between the two buildings. "It's coming out!" Carl yelled to the others.

As it emerged it reminded Eddy of watching a balloon being filled by a helium tank. The round bulbous head continued to expand and rise upward as it emerged from between the buildings and onto the street. Waves shimmered up the surface of the crystal clear beast, leaving its body larger each time. The translucent monstrosity finally set itself down on the street, resembling a twenty foot tall glass octopus with far to may arms. The creature stared at the four men through round transparent eyes, each the sizes of a buses windshield.

The see through octopus started to creep slowly forward, and Carl fired his gun, hitting it squarely in the center of one of the large clear eyes. Eddy saw the trail the bullet had left in the beast's body, leaving a small fractured tunnel several feet into its crystalline body before it finally stopped, the fired bullet clearly visible at the end of its narrow tunnel.

"It's solid" Eddy pointed out.

"Very solid" the gray skinned guard holding the gun acknowledged.

The octopus rose up slightly and all three men opened fire, all of their shots having similar results as the shot fired by Carl. The guard holding the little ball of lightning flung his arm forward and struck the monster in the top of the head. The purple electricity crackled as it hopscotched across the large smooth surface of the monster and then crawled across the outside wall of the near by buildings before dissipating. Half the surface of the things head was now spider webbed with cracks. The beast turned its head to look directly at the guard that had injured it. A shimmering wave ran over the surface of the beasts head, leaving its body again crack free, and gleaming once more. One of the see through arms swung out with the speed of a striking snake and hit the offending guard directly in the chest and sent him flying threw the air and into a near by office window.

The three remaining men opened fire, littering the beasts crystal like body with holes. The beast rose up several feet on its legs and charged directly towards them. The men jumped out of the way, but the see through monster did not seem to notice or care. It apparently had not been aiming for the officers at all, but for the delivery truck containing the captives from the raid. It wrapped several of its large see through arms around the large vehicle causing it to buckle in places. It quickly lifted the vehicle off of the ground and began sprinting down the street with alarming speed, until it finally grabbed hold of a fire escape and used it to quickly climb over a building and disappeared from view.

Eddy stared as he lowered his gun "Carl what was that?"

Carl continued to stare in disbelief, and then finally blinked as if he had just now remembered that Eddy was even there "I . . . honestly don't know" the man said.

Chapter 3

A Rose in the Garden

Edith and Xander where standing on a glistening wet concrete walkway. Edith knelt down to look at the small flowers that were growing happily a few inches from its edge. As she leaned over to look closer her long brown braided pigtails fell forward to rest on the damp dark earth next to her feet. Xander on the other hand just stood there staring up at the climbing vegetation of the jungle looking board as he fanned himself with his heavy coat in a futile attempt to keep cool in the hot hummed air.

"Why are we here again?" Xander asked. "I mean come on, we are the only ones here. No one comes to the Botanic Gardens in the winter."

"Which is a big part of why we are here. I can't grow everything myself you know, and with so few people here, no one will notice if I do a little, pruning of my own." Edith wiggled the tips of her fingers slightly, and several round seeds tumbled out from their seed pods and came whirling over threw the air to rest gently in her upturned hand. She looked back down and smiled at the pink flowers growing in front of her. "You know for someone that is dating a tree, you would think you would have a little more appreciation for plants."

"She is a dryad, not a tree. Ok she is sort of a tree. But she is a talking tree. Have you ever met a flower that can talk?" Xander asked.

"Yes, as a matter of fact, I have" Edith said.

Xander looked down at her in shock "where?"

Edith looked up at him and grinned "oh now you are interested in the flowers?"

Xander smiled, and then gave a nod towards the cluster of flowers that were in front of his sister. "Ok, all admit those are cool. The little pink stock things, make those flowers look like little flamingos."

Edith looked back down at the flowers in front of her "the pink stock things, as you called them, are called pistols, and yes they do make them look like flamingos." She then reached out and pointed to the little black sign that had white lettering etched into it that read flamingo flower.

Xander looked away sheepishly, a little embarrassed that he had not even noticed that the plants had signs on them. Suddenly he perked up "hey look, over there, it's Eddy." Edith quickly stood up and turned to see where her brother was looking, her long hair hitting her much taller brother in the stomach in the process. "I wonder what he is doing here."

They watched as Eddy stood on the edge of the path near the entrance and unzipped his brown leather bomber jacket. As they watched a tall woman with shoulder length sandy blond hair who was wearing a long white fleece coat came to stand next to him.

"Maybe he wanted to spend some time in a rainforest today as well" Edith said with a smile. "Who is that with him?" she asked as the woman put her arm in his.

"That would be Rose. Hey let's go say hi" Xander said, and began walking down the path in the direction of his friend before Edith even had a chance to respond.

Edith hesitated briefly before lurching forward to keep pace beside her brother. "That's Rose? Not exactly what I expected."

Xander chuckled "really, what did you expect?"

"I don't know" she stammered.

Xander glanced down at his sister as they walked. "Someone like you maybe?" he asked with a smile.

Edith's face flushed red "NO! Of course not" she blurted out a little quicker then she had intended, which caused Xander to laugh.

"Eddy, Rose, how is it going?" Xander called as they drew closer to the pair. "What brings you guys here?"

Eddy stopped talking to Rose and turned to wave at his approaching friends with a smile and then immediately began to walk towards them. "Wanted go some place warm" Eddy said.

"So you came to look at a bunch of stupid plants?" Xander asked with disbelief.

Eddy gave Xander a bit of a sideways glance. "You are the last person I would have expected to be badmouthing plants. Better not let Thena here you talk like that."

"You sound like my sister" Xander said with a laugh.

"Who is Thena?" Rose asked, having grown tired of not being part of the conversation.

Eddy smiled. "His girlfriend."

"Is she into plants or something?" Rose asked them.

Xander laughed again. "Oh yes, she is very into plants." Edith and Eddy joined in on Xander's laughter, leaving Rose to just stand there not understanding what they all thought was so funny.

Rose looked over at Edith and extended a slender hand that she could not help but notice smelled heavily of orange blossoms. "So I take it you are Thena?"

"Oh god no!" Edith said as she reached out to shake Rose's hand. "I am Edith. Xander's sister."

Rose looked at the tall dark man and then at the much paler and shorter woman standing next to him. "I never would have guest."

"We get that a lot" Edith said still smiling. "It is nice to finally meet you. Eddy has been promising to introduce you to me for a while now."

"Has he now?" Rose looked over at Eddy "so why have you been keeping us apart Eddy?"

"I haven't been keeping you apart. She lives in the Ken Carl area. It's almost a hour away. It's not like we can just swing by on our way to or from some place."

"So if she lives so far away, how did you two end up meeting?" Rose then looked over at Xander "or Xander, do you often drag your little sister places with you?"

"I dragged him along actually, and it is older sister, by six months anyways." Eddy made a mental note of the age difference between the two. It meant her birthday was in two months and he felt he should get her something. "We met over the summer actually. Xander introduced us when Eddy needed some help with . . . uh . . . something."

Rose's thin eyebrows rose up in realization "wait, I know your voice don't I." She quickly turned to Eddy "it was her voice I heard in the background of you phone over the summer. Back when you wouldn't see me for two weeks."

"It was not two weeks, but yes." Eddy held his hands up defensively as Rose began to fume. "Some people where after me as a result of a case I was working on, and I needed some place safe to hide. Xander figured that Edith's house would work. She is a friend who gave me a safe place to go when I couldn't go home."

Rose's eyes narrowed as she looked at Eddy. She then turned to Edith, and quickly changed her face to a pleasant smile. "Well thank you for giving him a safe place to stay. You know we really should get together sometime. I would love to get to know you better."

Edith smiled "how about tonight. My place. I'll make us all dinner." Eddy gave Xander a tens look, and Xander just shrugged.

Rose's smile broadened "sounds good. I look forward to it."

Rose's smile quickly faded as a unusually large ladybug came flying over. "Hello Eddy" the extremely small woman said as she came to hover in the center of the group. Eddy gave a small smile and slight nod, hoping Rose would not notice. Sara turned towards Edith and held out the tiny bag she had been caring to her. "I found the pollen you where looking for."

Sara suddenly darted upwards as Rose's hand came swinging towards her. "Blasted bugs" Rose said. "Eddy why do you attract so many lady bugs these day." Sara just stuck out her tongue and went over and landed on Edith's shoulder. "Ugh, it landed on you."

Eddy smiled weekly "sorry Rose doesn't like ladybugs."

"I can't believe you do" Rose said.

"Well we should get going" Edith said. "I need to go introduce my brother to a flower. I'll see you tonight. Eddy knows the way."

Eddy gave a little wave as they turned to walk away. When Edith and Xander were several feet away Sara finally spoke up. "That woman dose not like me one bit. To be honest the feeling's mutual."

"You don't' like Rose?" Xander asked. "But she is so nice."

"Maybe to you she is" Sara huffed. "But every time I come near Eddy when she is around, the woman goes nuts. I don't get her. Who doesn't like lady bugs?" She looked up at Edith "besides she smells funny."

"What you don't like the smell of citric fruit?" Xander asked. "I would have thought you would like it. It being all flowery and all."

Sara scowled "is that what that is supposed to be? What they grind the stuff up with, sulfur or something? She stinks!"

*   *   *

Eddy and Rose pulled into the driveway of the pale yellow house that was Edith's home. Some slight bits of faint green where still visible in the mostly brown grass of her front lawn. Eddy was nervous about tonight's dinner. It was not that he was nervous about the food, he had learned that Edith was a wonderful cook during the time he had stayed with her over the summer. No, he was nervous about having Edith and Rose in a room together all evening. He honestly did not know what Rose thought of Edith, or the fact that Eddy had been staying with her during the summer.

Rose's attitude could often change from disapproving to total acceptance as fast as if someone was flipping a light switch, making her often hard to read. He did however know that she had mistrust about how closed lipped Eddy had been about what was going on during their time away from each other, and now wondered if he had only made things worst in doing so. He now wondered if he should have simply told her the truth, mines the parts about magic that is.

Eddy rang the doorbell and Rose smiled as she held his hand. "This should be fun" she said. They looked at the door as they heard the lock disengage and the heavy wooden door swung open to reveal a smiling Xander.

"Xander what are you doing here?" Eddy exclaimed.

"Edith invited me" he said as the two stepped through the doorway. The tall man leaned over and whispered in Eddy's ear "she thought it might help things go a little smother."

"I am glade you are here" Eddy whispered back. "I really did not want to do this on my own."

Xander smiled and stood up straighter "dinner is almost done so I was told we should go ahead and take our seats."

The trio entered the dining room. Eddy pulled out a chair for Rose before taking one of his own next to her, and Xander took a seat across the table from him. The smell of food poured in from the adjacent kitchen and Edith finally entered caring a platter with a roast resting on it. She smiled at Eddy and Rose, but then scowled at Xander.

"I told you to tell them they could take a seat, not you. Now get your scrawny butt back in the kitchen and help me bring out the food."

"Why do I need to help?" Xander complained. "And don't say it's because I need to do more then just eat your food."

Eddy laughed and Edith smiled "I wasn't going to. They're my guests, and guests should not have to help serve the meal."

"I'm a guest too you know" Xander said.

Edith placed the platter in the center of the table. "You are family You don't count" she said before she turned and walked back into the kitchen.

"You know you better get in there" Eddy told him.

"I know, I know" Xander grumbled as he got up and walked into the kitchen.

Rose turned to look at Eddy "they have this conversation a lot?"

"All the time" Eddy laughed.

She hugged his arm and smiled "so where did you sleep when you stayed here. I want to hear all about it"

"Well" Eddy began "I slept down the hall behind the first door on the right. I slept on a futon, and shared my room with a bird named Arthur. Oh and I learnd how to sword fight."

"So that is how you got all those bruises" she said.

"Some of them. The darker ones where from when I finally found the man I was looking for. He beat me up pretty bad before we finally arrested him."

She smiled at him "well I am glad you made it through it all ok. I don't know what I would do with out you." She sat up and looked towards the kitchen as Edith and Xander came in caring food. "Thank you for looking after him for me" she said.

"Any time" Edith said. "Though not certain if I would be willing to let him stay over again. Talk about a high maintenance house guest. Taking care of him nearly killed me." Eddy, Edith and Xander began to laugh hared. Rose finally joined in on the laughter, even though she was not certain of why the comment was so funny to them.

"So any one else live here with you, other then the bird that is?" Rose asked Edith.

"I have a cat and a dog" she said. "There in the basement right now. Didn't want them getting in the way during dinner." Then as if on cue, Edith's orange cat came strolling up the stairs, and began walking towards them. "D'Artagnan, how did you get out?"

Rose turned around in her chair in order to see the cat. D'Artagnan looked up at her, and Rose smiled. "Well aren't you a pretty little cat" she said.

In response the cat arched its back and hissed. The hairs on its back and tail stood up on end, and then they began to lengthen, as the orange tabby began to grow in size, and its eyes began to glow orange like hot coals.

Edith and Xander looked at each other with panic stricken faces. The veil could not stop people from being able to see the cat increase in size. Eddy quickly grabbed a hold of Rose's face and kissed her. As he kissed her he quickly waved with his other hand for them to get the cat away. Edith quickly handed the dish she was holding to Xander, who nearly dropped it. She then ran over and quickly scooped up the cat, and rushed down the stairs with it. As soon as the cat was out of sight Eddy stopped kissing Rose.

"Sorry about that. He is normally not like this" Xander said as he awkwardly place the food on the table, spilling several peas across the table in the process.

"What do you mean? Eddy kisses me all the time" said Rose.

"I . . . um . . . meant the cat" Xander said.

"Did the cat do something?" she asked.

"Just got loose is all" Eddy said.

Chapter 4

Story Time With Swan

Carl had seemed to be trying to keep his distance from Eddy ever sense the night of the raid. Every time Eddy would walk into the same room as the giant, Carl would make a hasty exit. Many thoughts had raced through his head as to possible reasons. Was the seven foot tall giant embarrassed about having been brought to his knees by a pair of scrawny three foot tall men? Or was it that he had been saved from them by Eddy, a mere human. Then again it could be how it had all ended. Eddy himself could still not get his mind around the massive see through octopus. The thing had seemed invincible. Maybe if Eddy had managed to set something on fire? Everything had gotten really cold right before the creature had appeared, there just had to be a connection between the two.

Fire might have helped, but for some reason Eddy just could not seem to get anything to ignite, not sense the night outside the theater anyways. There had to be away to do it with out the people he cared about being close to losing their lives. He just had to find it. Given how Carl had been avoiding him, it had needless to say taken Eddy completely by surprise, when one afternoon he had found Carl sitting behind his desk and then suddenly been invited to join him for lunch.

As usual they had ended up at a waffle house across the street from the abandon rubber factory, a factory Eddy had no intention of every going near again. They had been at the restaurant for nearly ten minutes, and Carl had yet to say three words to Eddy. Finally the giant stopped polishing his fork and set it down and began to stare at Eddy.

"I think I need to tell you something" Carl said, then took a deep breath and continued. "The reason I have been avoiding you is I have been trying to decide how to tell you something. You are not going to like it." Eddy sat silently, patiently waiting for the man to get to the point. Eddy did not want to rush him out of fear that he might cause Carl to not tell him what had been on his mind all this time. "Remember how our little knocker friend we have in custody said something had happened to a guy named Travis?" Eddy nodded. "Travis Summers is the name of the man you saw Ezekiel Swan kill over the summer." This made Eddy sit up a lot straighter. Swan was a wight that he had been trying to track down in order to bring in for murder. An event that had led to him discovering the world of magic was real, and secretly all around him. The very man that he had squared off against outside of the theater just a few short months ago.

"There's more. I did a little more digging. From what I can tell Summers had ties to the group we raided few nights ago. After I made the connection I looked into Swan a bit more as well. Eddy, when you were looking at his record did you come across the only time he had ever been taken into custody by police?" Eddy nodded. "It mentioned that he had killed two other prisoners before he escaped. The two prisoners were a pair of grave robbers. Had a habit of selling their finds on the black market. They specialized in ancient artifacts Eddy."

"Leaving you to believe they were one of the suppliers for our little band of covert artifact dealers" Eddy interjected.

"Exactly" Carl said pointing a finger at Eddy enthusiastically. "This Travis Summers must have somehow messed up one of their deals, and Swan was sent to take care of him. Some sort of enforcer or something. Possibly was even their boss."

Eddy shook his head "I don't believe he is their boss. The wraiths they sent after me referred to him as their friend, not their boss."

"Wraiths, what wraiths?" Carl said a bit louder then he intended. He nervously looked around to see if any one had noticed. He was relived to see that no one had. "When did you tangle with wraiths?" he asked in a much quieter voice "and how did you manage to survive?"

"Just shy of two weeks before the run in with Swan outside the theater" Eddy told him. "I survived them because my next door neighbor came to my rescue."

"Your neighbor took out a group of wraiths?" Carl said with disbelief. "Who is your neighbor, Tabitha Vallen?" he said sarcastically with a small chuckle.

Eddy looked down shyly at the table for a moment before he looked up and with a uncertain smile said "yes, as a matter of fact she is."

Carl's jaw dropped in shock "your kidding?" Eddy shook his head. "Wow" Carl said with disbelief. After sitting silently for a moment so he could process what Eddy had just said, he finally began to speak again. "Any ways, back to the point at hand. Clearly our black market cheep artifact boys are tied to something bigger. The main question now is how do we proceed from here?"

"I think the next step is obvious" Eddy told him. "We interview someone close to it all. We talk to our prisoner."

Carl shook his head "no use. The knocker we had in my car won't share his box of Coco Krispies with anyone, let alone any info. He seems to be afraid of someone he only refers to as the blue lady. Who, or what for that mater, that is supposed to mean I have no clue."

"Not a lot of blue people are there?" Eddy asked.

"Barely any" Carl confessed. "Some nymphs, a hand full of sirens. That's about it. Your friend Crystal doesn't have a blue sister that works in organized crime does she?" he said jokingly.

"You would have to ask Edith, Crystal is her friend. But I highly doubt it. By the way, I was not suggesting we talk to the knocker. I meant we talk to Swan."

Carl nearly spit out his coffee from the shock. "You want to interview the man who tried to kill you? Are you crazy?" he said after he finally stopped chocking.

"No I am dead serious. During our fight he gave me the impression that he was part of something bigger. There where definitely bits that made it sound like he knew something. That there was more going on beyond the events I was wrapped up in. Besides if he won't talk to me, I can always threaten to beat him with a flaming piece of aluminum again." Carl just smiled.

* * *

Eddy walked up the long row of red concrete steps that climbed the low hill that the Colorado State Capital sat on. Despite the dark night sky Eddy could still see clearly do to the numerous lights surrounding the building. The large building very much resembling a scaled down version of the nations capital. The large strikingly white granite blocks loomed brightly in the night. Its large gold plated dome illuminated brightly by the numerous lights surrounding its base as it raised out of the roof top, making it look a little like a oversized yellow Christmas light.

As he drew closer to the stately structure he could see Carl standing at the base of the large granite stairs that marked the beginning of the building. Eddy's pace increased as he drew towards his friend. He was eager to find out what meeting him at eleven pm out side the sate capital had to do with talking to Swan.

"You made it" the giant called as Eddy stepped onto the large brick compass like landing.

"Yes" Eddy said as he came to stop in front of Carl who was now standing next to the large base of the Civil War monument. "Now why are we meeting here? I thought we were going to interview Swan?"

"We are" Carl said as he turned, and started walking towards the stairs and motioned for Eddy to fallow him. "He's here."

Eddy hurried after him. "Wait, what?" Eddy asked in utter confusion as he took only a brief glance at one of the three steps marked as being one mile above sea level, the letters carved deep into the stone. "Why is he at the state capital?"

"Because this is where the Seelie Court is. Well under it any ways" Carl said.

"Hold on. The Seelie Court is in the basement of the capital building?" Eddy asked with disbelief.

"No, of course not. It's under the basement. In the old coal tunnels" Carl clarified.

Eddy had heard once or twice about there being a series of old tunnels under the capital building that supposedly connected it to the surrounding government buildings. Story goes that they were at one point used to bring in coal in order to heat the buildings. But when coal had gone out of use, and been replaced by gas, the tunnels had gone out of use, or so Eddy had thought.

"So their in the tunnels?" Eddy asked.

"Why else would there be several miles of it down there?" Carl said as he turned his head to look over his shoulder at Eddy. As soon as he looked at Eddy however he came to an abrupt halt. "Oh boy. I thought this might happen."

"What might happen" Eddy asked as he turned and looked behind him.

Eddy's jaw hung open as he looked at what must be the thing Carl had been referring to. The large green bronze statue, that was built to honor the first Colorado Division of the Continental Army, had turned its head, and was now looking right at them. The large musket lowered, and pointed at the two officers as the statue dressed in a civil war uniform hopped down from its pedestal with a loud clank, and began to walk towards them.

"Good evening sir" Carl said trying his hardest to not sound nervous.

"Good evening Detective Strom" the statues voice rang out in a deep tone like that of a large church bell. "You are welcome to enter, but your human counterpart must stay here. Our world should stay hidden from their eyes."

"He is already aware of our world" Carl informed him. The statue looked at Eddy, eying him suspiciously. Eddy looked up at the metal guardian and gave a weak wave hello. "He can see you, and he knows you are moving." The statue looked at Eddy and then back at Carl.

"We are here to talk to Ezekiel Swan. It is important that we see him" Eddy told the living statue, the whole time looking out of the corner of his eye at Carl for any sign of support.

"Detective Shade had a first hand in the apprehension of the prisoner in question, and therefore is entitled to question him under statute thirteen of CDMA protocol. It does not discriminate against species."

The bronze giant shook its head disapprovingly. "This is unorthodox, but I will grant him entry. Proceed."

The statue jumped back up onto its pedestal and turned to once again face the street as Carl and Eddy proceeded to walk up the stairs. As they drew near the ornate doors of the capital Eddy looked back at the monument. "What was that?" he whispered.

"A type of golem. Many metal and stone golems guard things around the city. Along with a few foo dogs as well. We would use gargoyles, like in a lot of other cities, but they don't seem to like Denver's thin air."

"So that is why you tend not to see to many gargoyles on buildings in Denver" Eddy said.

Carl nodded as he stepped forward and pushed open the intricately carved wood door, and they walked into a wide hall with two rows of pillars running down the sides. The interior walls of the building were also made of granite but accented with a rare form of red marble known as rose onyx. They walked across the polished white floor and entered the central room of the capital. They approached a large oval shaped hole in the floor and Eddy leaned against the heavy brass railing. He looked up into the highest vaulted ceiling he had ever witnessed, rising 180 feet straight up, all the way into the top of the dome. He then looked down into the basements below. When he looked up again, he realized Carl was already on the move.

Carl led Eddy down one of the buildings central staircases, emerging on the level just below the stairs they had climbed to enter the building. After they reached the bottom Carl led Eddy around to the back of the stairs. Fixed in the back of the staircase was what looked like an ordinary office door, with the typical frosted glass window. Carl walked up to the keypad next to the door and punched in a code, then promptly pulled the doors polished handle to reveal a well lit staircase running parallel bellow the stairs they had just come down. He waved for Eddy to enter, and then quickly fallowed after him, closing the door behind him.

After a long flight of stairs they reached the white stone brick walls of the tunnels. Pipes and cables of varies sizes littered the passageway as they made their way through the bowels of the capital. The pipes were placed seemingly at random, giving no heed to where someone might be walking. Some ran across the ground, others sat high in the air, but more often then not, they sat at head level, or ran right through the middle, forcing one to crouch in order to proceed. They fallowed the tunnel for sometime before they came to a locked door in one of the walls. Carl produced a key and opened the door to reveal yet another staircase. They passed onto a short landing that led down even farther under the building. The staircase switched back and forth several times as the two made their decent below the city.

"So you bring the people you arrest right through the capital building? Doesn't anyone notice?" Eddy asked.

"Boy wouldn't that cause quite a scene" Carl said with a laugh. "No. During the day we use other entrances. This is just the only one open in the evening. The tunnels go on for some distance. Probably why Denver does not have a subway system."

When they reached the end of the stairs they entered into a short hallway that abruptly was blocked by a large brass metal plate with round fist sized rivets running around its boarder. Carl placed one of his large hands in the center and said something that sounded to Eddy like it could be the name of a dinosaur, and the metal plate slid silently into the wall. They walked through the new opening and continued down the hall. Eddy glanced back and saw the metal plate gliding back into place. He turned back towards Carl just as the hall widened dramatically. The long narrow room had walls lined with what at first glance looked to Eddy like stained glass, but under closer examination were revealed to be large sheets of smooth multicolored crystal. Each glowing with a light of their own. Periodically placed in the walls were stone arches housing solid looking wood doors.

"Welcome my friend, to the Central Annex of the Colorado Department of Magical Affairs" Carl said with pride. "You are probably the very first human to set foot in here in over a hundred years, if ever. Those double doors up ahead are the entrance to where the Seelie Court meet. Did your friends tell you about the Seelie?" Carl asked.

"A little bit. Their a group of elected officials, that essentially decide what's right and wrong in the world of magic" Eddy answered.

"That's one aspect of it. The court is comprised of some of the most powerful beings on the planet, and are charged with governing, and protecting the world of magic."

Eddy whistled "big job." Eddy suddenly came to an abrupt halt. "Hold on, are you saying that Denver is the center of power for the magical world?"

"No of course not. That's in England. Stone henge to be exact" Carl said.

"Then why is the court in Denver given so much power?" asked Eddy.

"Eddy, there is only one Seelie Court" Carl told him. "They preside over all jurisdictions in the wold. They travel from place to place when needed."

"Must slow down the court cases" said Eddy.

"Not as much as you would think" Carl said with a small smile. "We need to hang a left here, and go down a level to enter the prison block" Carl instructed him. "I called ahead so Swan should be waiting in an interview room for us."

They started down a narrow corridor. The sleek walls looked as if they were made of polished granite, much like the walls of the outside building more then sixty feet above them. After walking down the claustrophobic hall for some time, they reached a brass accordion gate that bared access to what looked like a giant bird cage hanging from a heavy chain. The cage hung in an alcove set in the wall, and dangled precariously above a dark hole just big enough for the cage to fit through. Carl slid aside the gate, and motioned for Eddy to enter the lift. Eddy complied, and stepped gingerly into the wire frame and Carl quickly stepped in after him causing the cage to dip slightly from his weight. He slid the gate shut, and they immediately began the slow decent into the hole with the chain clanking softly as it lowered them into the opening. For a moment, everything went black, and then a faint glow began to appear near their feet, and then slowly spread up their legs as they emerge onto the lower floor.

The prison level was no where near as charming as the previous level had been. Instead of crystal lined granite walls this floor contained walls of roughly hewed stone. The stone floor barely passing for flat in some places. Old 4X4's ran across the walls and ceiling. The whole appearance of the place reminded Eddy of a mine he had toured once in Idaho Springs.

They fallowed the cave like tunnels for a short distance until they came to a long desk sitting next to a large iron gate that completely blocked the rest of the tunnel. The polished redwood desk looked very out of place in the dark and dusty rock tunnel, the man behind it however did not.

The man was covered with thick pebbly gray skin. His long skinny arms resting atop the smooth wood, as his bony fingers regularly pressed together to form tall steeples. He had an under bite like that of a bulldog, and glared at them with pail yellow eyes as they approached.

"What can I do for you?" the creature said with a lisp, or maybe it was a hiss, Eddy could not quite tell.

"I am Detective Carl Strom" Carl said while holding out his ID. "We are here to speak with Ezekiel Swan. I called ahead."

The creature flipped through the papers on a clip board that had been resting on the edge of his desk. "Ah, so you have, so you have. He is waiting for you in interview room three." The man looked up at them "would you like to have a guard with you?" he asked.

"Is he shackled" Carl asked the man.

"Of coarse he is" the creature said defensively. "It is standard procedure for a criminal with his background."

"Then I see no need for a guard. One outside the door should more then suffice" Carl told him.

The pebbly skinned man got up, and walked up to the barred gate. He pulled a chain out from inside his shirt and inserted the intricate key that was attached to it into the lock. The lock made a loud clang, and the man pushed the gate open. Carl and Eddy walked through and the man immediately closed it behind them. The hall quickly opened up into a large oval shape room. The curved wall of the room was lined with evenly spaced heavy oak doors, each door standing about fifteen feet apart from the other and had roman numerals printed on them in faded white paint.

Eddy fallowed Carl over to the door marked with three I's, the roman symbol for the number three, and both men entered it. Inside, sitting in the middle of the brightly lit room, was Ezekiel Swan. The tall gangly man sat behind a low wooden table. His hands were chained closely together by a pair of large iron shackles. A pair of matching shackles were wrapped around the orange cuffs of his ankles. Another chain connected the two, as a large pin anchoring the center of the chain running between his feet to the floor. The man's long white hair was pulled back into a tight pony tail, making it easy to see the blood red eyes of the wight as they stared at them.

The wight smiled, making Eddy shudder, which in turn causing Swan's smile to broaden. Wights were predatory, and could literally smell fear. A fact Eddy was going to need to remember if he was going to make it through this. "Detective Strom, Detective Shade, how good to see you both again. I trust you are both doing well?" he said with an English accent.

"We are fine, and you? How is the food?" Carl asked, deciding to play along with the fake pleasantries.

"I've had better, but I have had worst as well. It is American food, all grease, no flavor. But it will suffice." Swan leaned forward, and rested his arms on the table as much as his restraints would allow. "Come on now, have a seat. Relax. We are all friends here." Carl took a seat at the table in front of Swan, but Eddy stayed standing. "Oh come on Edward, have a seat."

"We are not friends. You tried to kill me. You tried to kill my friends" Eddy shot back.

"And you burned my favorite suit. I think that makes us even, don't you? Now have a seat so we can get to why you are here" Swan said with a pleased smile.

Eddy reluctantly sat down in the chair next to Carl. "We need to ask you a few things. Specifically in regards to your employer" Carl said.

Swan leaned back in his chair looking pleased with the question and tried to put his hands behind his head, but then remembered that they were connected to his feet and that he could not, then decided to set them in his lap instead. "So you have finally come to ask the big questions. Ones you should have asked me months ago. This means only one thing. The dominoes are beginning to fall and you are beginning to see what is going on. Would you like me to fill in some blanks in the puzzle for you then?"

"How are you connected to Travis Summers?" Eddy asked him.

"I think you already know that one. I killed him of course" the wight said with almost a chuckle. "But I will assume you are referring to business wise, right? We shared the same employer, not the same station mind you, but we answered to the same people none the less."

"Why did you kill him?" Eddy asked.

"He lost something important to my boss. They were less then pleased needless to say, as you can imagine. So as her enforcer, I did my job" Swan said with a smile.

"And who is your employer Mr Swan?" Carl asked flatly.

"Oh that is a big question. The question of the century in fact it would seem. Might even blow your mind." Swan was clearly enjoying himself.

"I take it that means you won't tell us?" Eddy said, unable to hide his irritation.

"Oh no. I will tell you" Swan said with a chuckle. "And do not worry about if it is true or not. The dead do not tell lies."

"You were not sentenced to death" Carl pointed out.

"Wasn't I? I will either sit in this charming prison and die from the ghastly food, or I will eventually go free and be hunted down like a dog" Swan told them. "You see, they will assume I have talked rather I did or not. So I might as well talk."

"So who is the blue lady?" Carl asked him.

"Oh, so some fool has spilled a little already has he? Probably all part of the bread crumbs that led you back here to me. She is an elf. Her name is Cecelia Ballard."

"An elf that is blue? A blue elf!" Carl asked not able to hide his shock.

"Told you it would blow your mind. Oh and it gets better. She is the head of the UnSeelie Court." Swan leaned back in his seat with a look of complete satisfaction on his face, as he looked at the total disbelief that was now prominent on Carl's.

Carl regained his composer, and gave Swan a menacing look. "You are lying."

Swan continued to smile. "I told you, dead men don't lie. And I am about as close to a dead man as one can be, without actually being dead."

Eddy looked from Swan to Carl "what is he talking about? What is a blue elf, and what is the UnSeelie Court?"

"Oh poor Eddy" Swan simpered "thrust into a world you do not understand. Always having to play catch up." The weight leaned foreword as best he could and folded his hands together, and smirked. "So Detective Shade, how is the young lady that you took to the theater? You know the one that sucker punched me, and pulled all the air from my lungs. Your girlfriend wasn't she? Oh wait, she is not your girlfriend is she? That would be Rose, now wouldn't it?"

Eddy quickly stood up, causing his chair to fall backwards with a loud clang. "How do you know about Rose?" he demanded.

"Oh you would be surprised the things I know about you Mr Shad" Swan said as he leaned back in his chair looking pleased with himself.

Carl stood, and grabbed hold of Eddy's wrist. Eddy however did not even notice until he felt himself being pulled towards the door. "We need to go" Carl told him.

"Go where?" Eddy asked with his feet rooted in place, not wanting to leave the room. "Carl he knows about Rose. How does he know about Rose?"

"I don't know, but remember they also knew about Xander, but those are all questions for another time" Carl said while he still tried to pull Eddy towards the door. "I hate to say it, but right now we may have a bigger problem then how he knows people in your life. We need to go, and now?"

"Go where?" Eddy asked, never taking his eyes off of the smiling Swan as he was finally pulled through the door.

"To see the Seelie Court" Carl told him.

"Have a pleasant evening" Swan called after them as the door swung shut behind them.

Chapter 5

Coach Ride

Eddy had hurriedly fallowed after Carl down the tunnel and past the gate. The large man was moving like a man on a mission, walking fast, and making it very hard for Eddy to keep up. Something Swan had said had unnerved Carl. Eddy had no idea what it had been, and at the quick pace they were moving at, he had yet to find any opportunity to ask. All Eddy did know, was that Carl wanted to be someplace, and be there fast.

As the lift rose slowly Carl fidgeted impatiently, and Eddy finally received his opportunity to try and find out what was wrong.

"Carl whats going on?" asked Eddy. The man just stood there, staring as the next floor came into view as if he had forgotten Eddy was even there "Carl! What is going on?" Eddy asked even louder.

Carl finally looked at him, as he did so there was a hard look in his eyes. "What's going on? I was just told TWO, impossible things, and I have no way of knowing if they are true or not. If they are true, they could have a major impact on our world. And when I say our world, I do not just mean the world of magic." Carl stepped out of the lift and began walking down the hall at a much slower pace then before. "Given that most of what you know about magic is based on fairytales, or what has been thrust on you in the last three months I will assume a lot of what Swan said means little or nothing to you.

"The blue elves were one of the many elven subspecies. Their name comes from the obvious trait that they had blue skin. The blue elves are credited with being the fathers of human civilization. Not just modern civilization either. Civilization as a whole. Its very essence. They taught early humans how to craft tools. How to hunt and cook food. They gave mankind fire, and taught them how to make medicines. What herbs did what, that sort of thing.

"Make no mistake, they did not do this out of some sense of kindness. To them it was more like teaching a beloved pet a new trick. It amused them to see mankind play with the new toys they had given them.

"But with all the new knowledge came new wants, new desires, and in turn, war. The various tribes grew, and the larger ones grew into large civilizations, all driven by one thing. To have what someone else had. Wars broke out all over the world, and over the centuries the blue elves became a causality of those wars. In short Eddy, we were just told that an ancient being with a god complex is back from extinction, and running the UnSeelie Court."

"And what is the UnSeelie Court?" Eddy asked him.

"Something that was supposed to have disappeared towards the end of the Renaissance. Apparently that was just wishful thinking. Think back to all those fairytales you heard as a kid. Think of all the creatures that did things just to cause problems for the fun of it. Things that reveled in human misery. The antagonist in nearly every fairytale you have ever heard. That, is the UnSeelie Court."

"Oh" was all Eddy could say as they came to stand in front of a large set of dark wooden doors in the central annexe. The doors were framed in a thick stone archway that was carved of a single piece of gray stone. At the top of the frame were three relief carvings of closed eyes.

"We need to tell the Seelie" Carl said as he reached towards a large brass door knocker shaped like a three fingered clawed hand holding a large ring. He grabbed a hold of the heavy ring, pulled it out, and began to knock. "Rather the information is true or not, they need to be made aware of it."

"What do we do if they're not here?" Eddy asked as they waited in front of the large doors.

"I already know they won't be" Carl said. "They are rarely here unless we call for them."

"So how do we call for them?" Eddy asked, then he suddenly stopped talking. The three large carvings of eyes in the doors stone frame opened and revealed pale blue eyes that then slowly moved to peer down at the two men.

Carl looked up at the eyes, and stood up a bit straighter as he spoke. "I need to request an emergency meeting with the Seelie Court. I have recently received information of extreme importance that they need to be made aware of."

What information would that be? echoed through the heads of the men.

"It has to do with the possible return of their apposing court, and their association with a possible unregistered demigod" Carl told the door.

Eddy began to squirm as he had the sudden feeling of something crawling over his head, not on the out side, but on the inside of his skull. Almost like a shuffling of his thoughts. The sensation tingled, and hurt a little, but at the same time made him feel uncomfortably good. Then suddenly it was gone, and the eyes quickly closed, and a moment later the doors swung open, granting them accesses.

The large doors swung silently inwards, and a light blue glow flowed out. The room they entered was unlike any place Eddy had yet encountered sense entering the world beneath Denver. The rooms walls and floors were made of a solid dark wood. The surface of the room was seamless, as if it had all been made from a single piece of wood. The ceiling was made of an immense sheet of crystal that was emitting a constant warm light blue glow. Running along both sides of the spaciest room were neatly organized rows of padded pews, looking as if they belonged in a church. They walked down the central aisle towards a long tall podium. The polished wood podium stretched across the front of the room like a large alter. Seated behind the podium were seven large high backed chairs.

As they neared the front of the room a furry head appeared behind part of the podium. Eddy watched as a four foot tall man climbed up and stood on the top of its smooth surface. The man wore an ornate robe with golden tassels hanging from his sleeves. However, more then anything else it was the mans face that most drew Eddy's focus. He had ears set high on his head, but they hung down low to rest just past his shoulders. He had a slightly long face, with a small, light pink triangular nose set in the center, and he stared down at them with large round black eyes. To Eddy the man looked a bit like a cross between a rabbit and a man.

"What is that?" Eddy asked Carl.

"That is Yarow. The chambers caretaker" Carl told him.

The rabbit man crossed his arms over his chest and spoke, "the door let you in, and we know you can not lie to the door. It can read your mind, and would know if you were. So what do you need at this late hour?"

"We need to speak to the Seelie Court. We have recently gained information that they need" Carl told him.

Yarow stepped off of the podium and landed silently on the floor. "I suppose that means you want a transport?"

"Yes Yarow, if you would be so kind" Carl said with a smile.

Yarow gave a smile of his own as well. At least Eddy thought it was a smile, it was hard to tell with his rabbit like face. "That's why I am here after all. The worlds fastest taxi cab" Yarow said as he began walking to the far end of the chamber. "Well come on now. It is time for me to take you from point A to point B, with out moving a step."

Eddy looked over at Carl "what does that mean?"

"It means we are going to use the Coach of Morgan Mwyfawr. Yarow is it's keeper, driver, pilot. Not really sure what to call the one that operates the coach. Operator, that works" Carl said.

Eddy looked at him. Carl's answer had completely failed to answer Eddy's question. "What is the Coach of Morgan Ma . . . wa . . . ."

"That" Carl said pointing in front of them as a wooden panel in the wall slid aside to reveal a large golden egg the size of a mini van.

Yarrow placed one of his furry hands on the shinny surface of the enormous egg, and the metal seemed to shudder as ripples began running across the outside of the egg. Moving like ripples traveling across the surface of a pond, they radiated rhythmically outwards in neat little rings. Soon they began to not only radiate out from Yarow's hand, but began to ping outwards from multiple points across the surface of the giant gold egg with increased frequency

The metal began to peel away, rolling back on itself in thin curls, like that of wood being peeled away with a plainer. The center of the ripples all peeled away simultaneously, until the egg was left as nothing more then a standard egg shaped skeleton made of golden rod iron. The metal twisted and curved in beautifull and elaborate patterns, making it look like the surface of a Faberge Egg. Eddy had seen many spectacular things in the last few months sense his eyes had been opened to the world of magic, but this was by far one of the most beautiful.

"That is the coach?" Eddy asked in awe.

"That's it" Yarrow said gleaming with pride, like a teenager with a brand new sports car. "Want to take her for a spin? Or more of a jump I should say." Carl covered his mouth to stifle a laugh, and Yarow gave his a dirty look. "Hold the rabbit jokes, Detective."

"How is this going to take us to the Seelie Court?" Eddy asked as he looked closely at the structure as it sat snug in its stone alcove.

Yarrow smiled "it wont. It will bring it to you. Ever want to go to England Detective Shade? You are about to be there."

Eddy looked down at the little rabbit like man "I am afraid you have lost me somewhere."

"Oh relax. I haven't lost anyone in years" Yarow said jokingly, or at least Eddy hoped it was a joke. "The coach is a remarkable device. Once belonged to a welch king you know. It can take you to any point in the world you want to go in the near blink of an eye."

"It's a teleporter?" Eddy asked as he looked at the egg with a newfound wonder.

"Not quite" Yarow said. "A teleporter sends you someplace. The coach takes you there itself. But it's not a transport in the typical sense. You see, the coach never moves." Eddy looked even more lost, and Yarow seemed to be enjoying it. "The coach bends space" he explained.

"Bends space?" Eddy asked as he tried to wrap his mind around what Yarow had just told him.

"Think of it like a rubber band" Yarow told him. "Grab two ends of a rubber band, and pull it, it stretches out, right?" Eddy nodded. "Now when you let go, the rubber band pulls back together and the ends slam into each other" he said and clapped his hands together to emphasizes the point. "That is kind of how the coach here works. It allows the points of the world to collide with each other. For a moment everything occupies the same space, and during that moment, where the two points are one, it connects to another spot and clings to it, and as everything returns to its normal space, it leaves you there."

Eddy looked back at the coach. "Is it safe?"

"Of coarse it is safe. It you know how to use it. Which I do. Don't worry, I have a few hundred years of practice at this." Yarow stepped into the pointed end of the coach. "Now why don't we get going then?"

As Eddy and Carl stepped into the device the world outside appeared to twist and bubble, almost as if they were looking at it from underwater. Yarow placed his hands over a transparent control panel floating at the pointed end of the coach, and began to twitch his short furry fingers. The world around them began to ripple, and then Yarow suddenly thrust his hands forward and the wall in front of them came rushing towards them. Eddy cringed, but instead of hitting the wall, they passed through it, and the world around them went dark.

Before Eddy knew it, they were moving down a long mine shaft, then suddenly they passed through another wall. For a moment they were passing through a massive cavern adorned with enormous stalagmites and stalactites and the walls were covered with beautiful stone waterfalls. They seemed to travel mid air through the cave, passing through many of the stone structures as they made their way. Eddy looked up and the entire world flowed down towards him like water rushing down over the edge of a great waterfall. Buildings, trees, streets, mountains, and endless prairies, all came rushing forward at once, as if to spill over and drowned him. The feeling made him feel sick, and he had to look away. When Eddy looked behind them all he saw was the wall of the alcove they had started in, still sitting motionless behind them. When he turned around to face forward once again, they were under water with a human sized catfish swimming towards them. Then suddenly everything went black again.

Suddenly the world grew bright as they passed through deep blue water. They moved through the water breathlessly for what seemed like forever, but in reality was only seconds. On the way they passed through a pod of whales, and then a sandy shore, and then suddenly the coach was resting in an alcove in the wall of a stone chamber.

Chapter 6

The Seelie Court

The walls of the chamber were constructed of large gray blocks that stretched far up into the air towards a vaulted ceiling with its crisscross of wooden rafters. The smooth stone floor was covered with a series of expertly woven rugs. Running across the far end of the room was a large empty banquet table. The room made Eddy think of the great hall of a castle. A ring of thick, large pipes of varying length hung in a circle from the rafters, and a human sized medal tear drop hung suspended by some unseen force in there center. As the trio stepped from the coach and into the room, the tear drop began to move, striking the pipes, and causing them to play a melodic tone. One of the many doors that lined the left wall swung open, and an enormous frog with elongated front legs hobbled out of it. Its eyelids blinked over enormous golden eyes as it gazed at Eddy.

The creature dashed towards them in awkward loping strides. It stopped abruptly in front of them and sat up on its hunches almost like an enormous prairie dog or rabbit. "What is the meaning of this?" bellowed the frog as it stared down at Yarow and flapped a pair of fins on the side of its head that were positioned like ears. "Why have you brought a human here?"

A fairy with a double set of metallic blue wings fluttered over and landed on the frogs head and yawned. "What is going on?" she asked sleepily.

The frog rolled his eyes up in a futile attempt to look at the top of his head. "Yarow has brought a human to our home."

"This human is Detective Edward Shade, and is the man that was instrumental in the capture of one Ezekiel Swan" Carl said. "We have recently been interviewing Swan in relation to another case, and have gained information that may be of vital importance, and request an audience with the Seelie Court in order to share it with them."

"Dose this matter require the attention of the whole court?" the large frog asked.

"It would be preferable your honor" Carl told him.

"Interesting" said the small woman sitting on top of the frog mans head.

"Yes Solice. I am most curious to hear what information a convicted murderer provided that would warrant the attention of the entire court."

"No, not that Douglas." Solice lifted off from Douglas' head and came to hover directly in front of Eddy's face. "The human can see us. This human has the sight."

"Why do little people with wings always hover so close to my nose?" Eddy asked Carl.

Solice smiled the put both her diminutive hands over her mouth as she began to giggle with excitement. "I was right? He can see us!"

"Eddy mind your manners" Carl reprimanded. "These are members of the Seelie Court."

"Sorry" Eddy said sheepishly.

Solice began waving her hands back and forth apologetically. "No, no. It's ok."

"No offense your honor, but could you please back up just a little? It is starting to make my eyes hurt" Eddy said as his eyes began to blink uncontrollably and started to water.

Solice quickly backed up a few feet. "Sorry about that Detective . . . Shade was it?" Eddy nodded. "It is so rare to encounter a human who has the sight. I may have gotten a little over exited. Forgive me. How in the world did this happen to you anyway?"

"It is a long story" Eddy said. "It's actually connected to the man we talked to tonight."

The conversation was interrupted as one of the doors opened and what looked like an enormous hyena strolled into the room. As the massive animal, who seemed to be wearing blue jeans and a yellow button up shirt, walked across the room it suddenly stood up and placed both of its paw like hands over its ears.

"Will someone turn off those blasted chimes? Six AM is far to early for visitors. I only got to bed three hours ago" the large gnole whined pathetically.

A women with jet black hair who looked like she might be from India peaked out from around a door frame. "Oh for crying out loud Brian quit your wining. It is no ones fault but your own that you were out partying all night. Not every one needs to adjust to your ridicules schedule." The woman then slithered out on an enormous red snake tail. "Right Max?" The snake women asked the stunning tall Asian woman with long light blue hair that ran down to the center of her back that had also entered the room.

"Indeed Ahalya." The Asian woman said in a soft spoken voice. "We appreciate your desire to have fun, but you do have responsibilities."

"Responsibility dose not mean you don't get to have fun" said a sing song group of voices. When Eddy turned he discovered that the voices did not come from multiple people, but from a single source, a four foot tall light golden furred fox. "I have always believed you can make time for both" the fox said in synchronized voices, one to match each of its nine tails.

"Oh most defiantly Kitsune" said a child's voice from behind the two officers.

Eddy spun around to find the space behind him was empty. He noticed Yarow leaning against the wall by the alcove that the coach was resting in. Yarow smiled and politely pointed a furry finger towards the ground. Eddy looked down and jumped, nearly falling backwards in the process. Standing in front of him, just a little taller then his knee was a dusty colored gray coyote.

The coyote looked up at him and gave an almost human like grin, and snickered. "That never gets old" it said in its child like voice.

"Kaiouti, stop that" said a deep chocolaty voice with a heavy accent from across the spacious room. Eddy whirled around and watched as a tall man with tanned skin and the head of a hawk strolling across the room towards them. "One would think that after ten thousand years you would have grown up at least a little by now."

As the coyote strolled past Eddy it stood up and transformed into a eleven year old Native American boy wearing blue jeans and a t-shirt. "And one would think you would have learned to lighten up Bakari."

The woman with the light blue hair shook her head. "Enough! I am certain that our visitors came here for a reason, and it wasn't to hear us bicker like children." When she looked at Eddy a small amount of surprise showed on her face.

"Yes Max" Solice said "he is human, and yes he can see us. Your blue hair and all. So are you enjoying the real world?" the little fairy asked Eddy.

Max smiled "interesting. But some how I doubt that is why they are here."

Carl cleared his throat in order to get the rooms attention. "Earlier this evening we were interviewing a convicted murderer known as Ezekiel Swan. During the interview he revealed to us vital information about his employer."

"And why is this relevant to us?" Douglas asked.

"He was working as an enforcer for the UnSeelie Court" Carl said with the most serious tone Eddy had ever heard him use.

The gnole let out a low growl. "Impossible? The UnSeelie court was wiped out hundreds of years ago. They are extinct."

"Your honor, I know that has been our long belief. Rather this is the UnSeelie of old, or a new organization by the same name, I do not know. I do however believe the information we received is indeed credible." Carl paused a moment before he continued. "There is more . . . I do have good reason to believe that this is indeed the original UnSeelie. Swan also told us a bit about the nature of the groups leader." Carl paused and took a long breath before he continued. "They are taking orders from a blue elf."

The room fell silent. It was Solice, who finally broke the silence. "Detective . . . are you certain?"

"Unfortunately, yes" was all Carl said.

Kitsune looked around the room "this is not good news" the multiple tailed fox said in its nine voices. Eddy raised his hand hesitantly and Kitsune looked at him. "Detective, if you have a question, then ask it. You do not need to raise your hand for permission."

Eddy quickly put his hand back at his side, feeling more then a little embarrassed. "I am afraid I do not fully understand the problem here. I get why this UnSeelie Court would be of concern, Carl explained that they are trouble. But why is this blue elf of so much concern?"

Brian strolled forward and looked down at Eddy. Eddy could not help but shrink back a little. The gnole was immense. He towered over even Carl and one could easily see the massive muscles bunching and rippling under his short fur as he moved. Then of course there was his head, with its long mouth filled with pointed teeth.

"Did our friend here not explain the history of the blue elves?" he asked.

"Yes. They essentially created human civilization" Eddy said.

"And then were wiped out, or so we thought, during wars between humans. Wars mind you that they started for their own amusement" Brain finished. "There are regrettably many conceited creatures from the world of magic, but none have been worst then the blue elves. To them, every living thing existed for their own amusement. They saw the world as nothing more then their play thing. Do you understand now why ones existence would be of concern, and why it being in charge of a group who's whole purpose for existence, is to cause other living things misery, makes this an even larger problem?"

"Then there is their power" Ahalya hissed. "I do not know how much you know of our world, but what do you know of the use of magic?"

"That all living things have the potential to use it" Eddy said "and that we all have a particular dominant element that we can call on."

"Very good" Ahalya said with a smile. "This will be easier to explain then I had feared. You see, Eddy, was it?" Eddy nodded. "What you said is correct. All except for one part. You see Eddy, some people can call on more then one element. Some are even standing in this very room" at that she nodded towards Max, who looked away shyly. "The blue elves can call on all four of the base elements. Some can call on the sub elements as well. This in short, makes then creatures of almost god like power. In fact many ancient civilizations thought that was exactly what they were. Story's of gods creating the human civilization, pulling them from the darkness, endowing them with knowledge or fire. That was them."

"It wasn't always them" Kaiouti grumbled.

"I said almost. Forgive Kaiouti's complaint. He gave the people of North America many things. Yes, some of them were headaches, but some were good as well" Ahalya said.

"Some really good headaches" Kaiouti snickered.

"I think I understand now" Eddy said solemnly.

"We have at least one more known member of the organization in our custody" Carl said. "A knocker named Albert Tarsh. I have not been able to get any information from him, short of that he is scared to death of a blue woman which we can only assume means a blue elf named Cecelia Ballard. One of you may have more luck."

"How did you come by this Tarsh fellow?" Bakari asked.

"We arrested him during a raid on a group that has been smuggling artifacts into the city of Denver" Carl told them.

"What would the UnSeelie want with a bunch of artifacts?" Douglas questioned.

"That we don't yet know" Carl told him.

"Was Tarsh the only one you arrested?" Douglas asked.

"We had six others" Carl told them. "Sadly, the others, and the CDMA truck they were in was taken by . . . a large see through octopus."

"Fascinating" Max said from behind the others. Everyone in the room turned to look at the woman whose pale face flushed red at the sudden attention. She clearly did not like being everyone's center of focus.

"Do you know what it is?" Douglas asked her.

"Possibly" Max said. "Keep me posted if you encounter any more, see through monsters. Do you have any more information for us?"

"Sadly, no" Carl said.

"Then we shall wish you good day. Or is it good night for you two?" Solice said. "I always have trouble with time zones."

"You have given us much to think about" Max said. "Keep us posted of any new information, and we will be certain to do the same."

Carl nodded, said a quick thank you, and began walking back towards the coach. Eddy gave a quick nod of his own, and hurried after the giant.

Chapter 7

Lions in Denver

Carl, Eddy and Yarow were speeding through a forest, passing straight through the massive trunks of trees, then suddenly they were floating through a vast ocean. After that they passed through a cave, then a lake, a mine, and finally arrive in the court chamber they had left from earlier that evening. They stepped out of the coach and Yarow grabbed hold of Eddy's arm with one of his furry paw like hands and stopped him.

"Wait" Yarow said softly. "I have something for you." He reached inside of a pocket on the side of his robe and produced a small round translucent blue stone about the size of a nickel with a strange symbol, almost like an overly geometric letter, floating on the inside. "Max wanted you to have this."

Eddy looked down at the small blue ball. "What is it?"

"Think of it like a magical cell phone. It will allow you to contact Max if you learn anything new" Yarow told him.

Eddy took and marble like object and put it in his pocket and then looked at Yarow. "So Max can use more then one element?" Yarow nodded. "So what is she anyways?"

"I have known Maxine for a long time" Yarow began "and I do know what she is, however I will not tell you. She prefers to keep that to herself, so it's only her place to tell. I will tell you that her kind were once very heavily hunted. Hunted to the brink of near extinction. But don't let not knowing worry you, you can trust her. Now you two have had a long night, I suggest you go and get some sleep."

Eddy and Carl made their way across the annex and back into the tunnels that would lead them back up to the lower level of the capital building.

As they walked Eddy pulled the large blue marble back out of his pocket and watched the rune inside slowly drift silently inside. "How do I use this thing any ways?" he asked Carl.

"I have no idea" Carl told him as he looked down at the object in Eddy's hand. "I have never seen anything like it. She must like you."

Eddy looked at the translucent ball one more time before he put it back into his pocket. "So now what do we do?"

Carl placed his hand on the door and commanded it to open. "We go home and we get some sleep, just like Yarow told us to. In the morning I will put in some calls. Look into some possible leads. See if I can connect any more dots." Carl let out a long sigh as they emerged on to the upper landing outside the building. "I will let you know if I learn anything and we will go from there."

They walked in silence as they went down the large granite staircase and walked past the silent bronze statue and they made their way to the street below. Finally they reached the vacant road.

"Well then I suppose I will see you at work then" Eddy said as he zipped up his coat to try and hold out the cold. "It sure got cold while we were in there" he said with a shiver.

"Yeah, it did" Carl said. The two men suddenly looked at each other, as the same thought entered their heads simultaneously. They both looked back and forth down the street for any signs of anything that might be on its way to attack them, but relaxed when they did not see anything.

"This whole thing has me jumping at shadows again" Eddy said.

Carl laughed "Hey, all because you are paranoid, doesn't mean that they are not out to get you."

Eddy smiled, and then Carl suddenly vanished from view, fallowed by an immediate thud and a fast dragging sound. Eddy frantically looked around until he saw Carl laying several feet away with a large see through lion pinning him to the ground. Carl was trying to push the beast off of him, and despite the fact that the lion had to scramble with its back paws in order to stay in place, Carl did not seem to be making any headway.

Eddy began running towards the giant, but then froze in his tracks as he heard a reverberating roar come from directly behind him. He quickly turned around and saw another lion coming his way. It plowed into him with tremendous force and sent him rolling across the ground. The lion pounced for him, but Eddy rolled to the side, narrowly escaping its enormous claws. The beast let out another roar that sounded like it was echoing through a long tunnel. Eddy looked back and saw that the transparent animal was still far to close for comfort.

Eddy began to crawl frantically across the street, but did not get very far before the lion grabbed him by the leg and began to drag him backwards, its sharp teeth digging deep into him as it pulled him helplessly across the frozen asphalt. Eddy caught a glimpse of Carl and saw that he had managed to get his hammer out, but could not seem to get a good enough swing to do any real damage to his attacker. The hammer was hitting the lions side with about as much efficiency as a pebble trying to drive in a railroad spike.

"Set them of fire!" Carl screamed at Eddy.

"I can't" Eddy complained.

"Yes you can. I have seen you do it. That metal bar you used to fight off Swan. Do it again" Carl screamed.

"I can't! I've tried, but I just can't get it to work again!" Eddy said almost sobbing.

His powers had worked before when there was a real need. When peoples lives were in danger. He had a need now, but why could he not get it to work. Carl and him were going to be ripped apart by a pair of prismatic lions, and all because of his ineptitude. Suddenly Eddy had a thought and spun himself around to look at the lion as it dragged him. He got his free leg underneath him and kicked back hard at the ground and tore himself free. The force ripped his pant leg and left deep gashes in his leg, but more importantly he was loose, and upright as well. He quickly reached for his gun and pointed it at the lion. Without even taking aim he fired at the creature and the head of the lion exploded into a fine white powder with a deafening pop. Suddenly another loud shot rang out and the middle of the creature exploded as well. Eddy stood stunned, he had not fired the second shot. Two more shots rang out and Eddy looked over to see Carl covered in thick blanket of white.

"Are you all right" a metallic voice called to them. Eddy spun around and saw the bronze statue walking towards them, smoke drifting lazily up from the muzzle of his musket.

"Yes, I think so" Eddy said as he held out his arm to let some of the white powder drift down to land on his hand. He recognizing it in the brief moment before it melted away. It was snow. Eddy looked over towards Carl and saw the giant was making his way over to meet him. Eddy knelt down next to one of the remaining glassy limbs and touched it. It was cold, so cold that it made his skin burn. The leg was made of solid ice.

Carl ran up behind Eddy. He was breathing hard from being out of breath, and he had to take several deep breaths before he managed to speak. "Eddy are you ok?" he finally managed to get out.

"I am fine, really" Eddy took a step forward, but fell when he tried to put pressure on his injured leg. He would have fallen to the ground if not for the arm of the bronze man that caught him.

"That leg is rather torn up. We should get you inside so someone can look at it" the bronze man said. At that he picked Eddy up off the ground and began carrying him inside while cradling him like a baby.

"To be honest" Carl said as he fallowed behind "I am surprised that thing didn't tare your leg clean off."

Eddy reached inside his shirt and pulled out the little velvet black bag that he always wore around his neck. "You know it is not the first time I've survived an attack that should have killed me."

"What is that?" Carl asked curiously.

"It is a pouch containing numerous protective charms" the bronze man said without ever looking at it.

"Edith gave it to me" Eddy added as he looked at the bronze man wondering how he knew what it was.

"Really? I will have to remember that" Carl said. "Where did she get them?"

"She told me she made them" Eddy told them.

"Handy person that friend of yours" was the last thing Eddy heard Carl say as he passed out and was carried through the ornate doors of the capital.

Chapter 8

Stillwater

Eddy's head felt like it was swimming. As his mind swam back to the surface, he kept getting hit with frequent waves of nausea. Finally he became vaguely aware that something hard was pressed against his back and head. Bright lite began to spill in through his eye lids. He began to feel woozy, and tried to sit down, only to discover that he was in fact lying on his back.

"Woe, hold on there Detective. Don't try to move" came a muffled voice that sounded like it was coming at him through a pair of distant, cracked speakers.

"Where am I?" Eddy finally managed.

"My office" said the voice, sounding clearer and clearer with every word. "I am Doctor Stillwater. I am going to fix your leg."

"What happened" Eddy asked, as he attempted to open his eyes.

"What do you remember?" the voice asked him.

Eddy finally managed to open his eyes, but saw nothing but the over head lights of the office. "Lions made of ice. One grabbed my leg. I tried to pull away . . . I don't . . . know what happened after that."

"You got free" Doctor Stillwater told him. "Tore up your leg pretty bad doing so to. The Kernel took care of your ice lions. After you passed out he carried you inside."

"Who?" Eddy asked.

"The guardian" said the voice as he came to stand next to Eddy.

Doctor Stillwater was tall, with a head that seemed a slight bit larger then it should have been. He was covered in gray fur, except for around the eyes, those were ringed in white, like a reverse raccoon, and he had a pair of black stripes running across his cheeks. His long snout smiled to reveal interlocking triangular teeth. There was something familiar about the man, but Eddy had trouble remembering what it was. He new the man, somehow reminded him of something he had seen on a vacation to Arizona when he was a kid, but he just could not put his finger on what it was.

Eddy looked down at his leg, and saw the deep red gashes running through it, within the red there were thinner little streaks of white in the middle. Eddy realized the lion had torn him down to the bone, and he suddenly felt woozy as he looked at it. He forced himself to look away, and focused on the doctor instead.

"So what happens now?" Eddy asked him, despite being afraid to hear the answer. Deep down he knew the answer was likely going to be he would loose his leg. At the very least he would never walk again.

The doctor picked up a bundle of eagle feathers, and a rattle that was made from an old dried out squash, and held them in one of his enormous furry hands. He glanced at Eddy's leg casually. "Oh you will be fine. Mostly just muscle damage." He picked up a bundle of sage, and then lit the end of it on fire by holding it over a nearby candle. "Give me a few minutes, and you will be as good as new, and then you will be able to drive yourself home."

"But, but . . . my leg is shredded down to the bone" Eddy stammered.

"Little past in one spot. If you were standing where I am, you would see just a little bit of marrow" the doctor said with a chuckle, the smile on his face made him look like an angry badger. "But no worries. I'll patch you up as good as new. Won't even be much scaring." He walked around the exam table to stand directly over Eddy's mangled leg. "Now just relax. Your leg will tingle and itch while I do this. It will feel kind of like ants are crawling on it. Just try and hold still." The man raised his hands over Eddy's leg, then stopped to look at him. "If you want, I can strap you down? Some people find it helps."

Eddy shook his head. "No, I'd rather not."

"Suit yourself" Doctor Stillwater said. He began shaking his hand with the feathers and rattle rhythmically over Eddy's leg, while waving the burning sage in a swooshing motion close over his wounds. The gashes began to itch, and then crawl. The skin around the wound didn't just feel like something was crawling on it, it felt more like something was crawling out of it.

Eddy dared to look down at his leg, propping himself up on his elbows so he could see better. Little pink bubbles formed on the edges of the tears, rising and popping in a frothy mess. As Eddy watched, he noticed that only the bubbles on the outer edge were popping as new ones formed on the inside edge. As each bubble rose, another one would pop, exposing shiny skin below it. Eddy then realized the wounds in his leg, were slowly shrinking.

Eddy became so entranced by the sight of his leg being remade by the foam, that he completely forgot about the crawling sensation that it caused. Finally the foam around the now small lines fizzled a little, and then stopped.

The doctor picked up a towel and wiped off Eddy's leg, the only evidence of the massive gashes now, were small scars, no thicker then a pencil line. He sat up and pulled his leg closer, and ran his hand over the moist smooth surface."

"Don't worry, the hair will grow back" Doctor Stillwater said. "Skin, muscle, bone, that I can regrow. Hair, I can't. Go figure" he said with a shrug.

"That is incredible" Eddy said, still staring at his leg.

"Ah, that's nothing" Doctor Stillwater said. "Simple Kachina medicine. Nothing to it."

"Kachina? Is that what you are?" Eddy asked as he looked over at the man.

"Yep" the doctor said with a toothy smile.

"I think I saw a statue of you at a gas station in Arizona once" Eddy told him.

"Really?" said the doctor with another toothy grin. "Did they get my good side?" he asked, then struck a pose like a model on the end of a runway.

Eddy could not resist laughing. "No, they didn't" at that the doctor joined in on the laughter.

Chapter 9

Magic Marble

Eddy found himself once again sitting in Edith's kitchen. He sat on the long wooden bench that ran along the wall behind her kitchen table. Edith poured two glasses of lemonade then walked over and set one of them in front of Eddy before taking a seat of her own across from him.

"So what brings you down to my neck of the woods" Edith asked him before taking a sip of her drink.

Eddy yawned, then looked at Edith apologetically. "Sorry. I haven't had a chance to get any sleep yet. I had quite the night."

"Really, how so?" Edith asked him.

"Well I was attacked by lions in downtown to start with . . . or more to end with I suppose would be more accurate. Maybe I should start at the beginning" Eddy said.

Edith smiled at him. "Yes, that might be a good place to start."

"Well, Carl took me to see Swan last night" he told her.

"And what did that spineless dirt bag have to say?" Edith asked with disgust.

Eddy looked at her and raised one of his eyebrows. "Someone holds a grudge now don't they." Eddy took a sip of his lemonade, and nearly chocked. "Wow? So not your normal recipe." Eddy opened his parched mouth and smacked his lips. "I think you forgot to sweeten it" Eddy set his glass down on the table. "Well, at least I am awake now. Anyways, he told us that he was working for a group that calls themselves the UnSeelie court, and that it is being run by something called a blue elf. Carl was pretty upset by all of it, so he took us to go see the Seelie Court."

"Swan told you all that, and then you actually went and talked to the Seelie Court?" Edith said as she nearly jumped out of her seat.

Eddy smiled at her obvious look of surprise. It was nice to be the one surprising her for a change. "Yeah, incredible isn't it. Oh that reminds me" Eddy leaned over to the side and began to dig around in his pocket. "A woman named Max gave me this in order to stay in touch with her. I still need to tell her about the ice lions last night." Eddy held out the blue marble with the floating rune in it, so he could show it to Edith.

Edith reached out in order to touch it, but then drew back. "How dose it work?"

"To be perfectly honest, I have no idea" Eddy said. "Sadly it didn't come with instructions. To tell the truth, I don't even know what it is. Do you?"

"No idea. Never seen anything like it" Edith said shaking her head.

You are already using it said Max's voice.

"Did you hear that?" Eddy asked.

Edith looked confused "hear what?"

Eddy looked at her and scrunched up his brow "Max. I swear I just heard Max."

She can not hear me Eddy. Only you can Max told him.

"How" Eddy asked.

Because of what you are holding in your hand. Only those touching the, Max took such a long pause that Eddy thought that he had lost her. *Sphere* she finally said. *It connects you to me.*

"She is talking to me through the blue marble thing" Eddy finally told Edith as he suddenly realized that it looked like he was talking to himself, and that he better fill her in on what was going on before she started to think he had finally lost his mind. "Only I can hear her because I am the only one holding it."

Edith reached out to touch the faintly glowing blue ball. *Don't let her touch me!* Max's voice said frantically in Eddy's head. Eddy was confused, and as Edith continued to reach for the sphere, Max's voice range through Eddy's head again. *Don't let her touch the sphere. I only want to talk to you.*

Eddy closed his hand and drew it back, and Edith looked at him confused. "She said she only wants to talk to me" he explained.

"Oh" Edith said as she leaned back in her chair, looking more then a little hurt.

You discovered something new about the translucent creatures said Max's voice. *The octopus, and . . . lions?"*

"Yes, but how did you know that? How did you know about the lions? That only happened just a few hours ago" Eddy said unable to hide his shock.

I can see it in your mind. As long as you are in direct contact with my, sphere, are minds are connected. Many of your thoughts are open to me. I try and keep to only the ones you direct at me, but sometimes those thought are directed before you have time to say them. Your words are really just a triviality when it comes to this form of communication Max told him.

So you can hear me now? Eddy thought.

Yes. Quite clearly. Now the beasts, they were made of ice weren't they? came Max's words.

Yes Eddy said. *Did you pull that from my mind?*

Sadly, no. I had my suspicions already, but felt I should keep them to myself until more was known. The ability to make constructs from ice, especially large, and independently moving ones, is quite rare Max said. *Who ever made them must be quite powerful.*

You mean they are not real animal, they are the result of someone using magic? Eddy asked her.

Yes, they are most definitely magic made monsters, and their creator clearly is not on our side. What is worst, is they seem to be aware of who you and Detective Strom are Max said. Eddy looked at Edith. *You are worried about her, about her safety.*

Yes Eddy told her.

As long as they do not know about her, she should remain safe Max reassured him. *I can tell you care deeply for her.*

In the short time I have know her, she has quickly become one of my closest and most trusted friends Eddy told her.

Hmm, friend. I suppose that word works Max said.

Swan knows about Edith Eddy reminded her.

True, but besides you and Detective Strom, no one has come to visit him Max said. *But if your concern is so great, maybe a guard would help put your mind at rest* Max suggested.

I don't think she would go for that Eddy told her.

What would you suggest? she asked him.

Maybe my friend Sarafin can keep an eye on her. That is why Thena had her fallowing me last summer. In order to help me out if I got into trouble Eddy thought.

Thena? Oh Lady Thena, Thena of the willow tree. If she has assigned a guardian, then I am certain that they will be more then adequate Max said.

Along with the words he felt a strange sensation come across his face. It felt like he was smiling, but it was not his face that wore the smile.

You know Thena? He asked.

Of course. We go back a very long way. Sadly however I have not seen her, or even heard her name in far to many generations. Max's thoughts felt happy and pleasant as they rolled through Eddy's head. Suddenly her mind took on a much more serous edge. *Do not worry your friend Edith with details of your evening last night. There is no need to worry her unnecessarily.*

But she might be able to help snapped through Eddy's thoughts before he could stop them.

In time, maybe. I sense she has been of great help to you in the past. If the need for her help seems worth the risk, then I will trust your judgment Max said. *We have know each other for not even half a day, but I can sense in your heart that you are a good man. You are also clearly a wise one to know that you can not do things on your own. Be careful. Trust your instincts. Powerful enemies are making plans, and like it or not you have become a part of them. If you need me, do not hesitate to contact me again. Now place me back in your pocket to sever the connection.*

Eddy complied, and inserted the strange blue marble back into his pocket. As soon as he let go of it his mind was instantly his own once again. He looked across the table at his friend, now not at all certain what he should do.

Edith looked at him expectantly. "So what did you two talk about?" she asked him with a smile.

Eddy smiled back uneasily. "I was just filling her in on what had happened last night."

"So what was it you were saying about the Seelie Court and, lions in downtown?" Edith asked him.

"You know what, don't worry about it. Everything turned out fine" he said as he got up from the table. "You know I should probable get going. I've been up for over twenty four hours now."

"You can always crash here if you want" Edith offered.

"No that's ok" Eddy told her. "I still need to report in at the station. Work day and all. Besides I need to see if Carl found out anything else."

Edith fallowed him as he made his way to the door. "Do you want me to come with you?"

"No, that's ok. Besides don't you have work today?" Eddy asked.

"Oh, yeah. Of course. See you later" Edith called as Eddy walked out the door and got in his car.

Chapter 10

Envelope

Eddy found himself sitting on his couch, leaning forward on his knees and staring at the legal size envelope in his hand. He had been home for the past two hours, most of that time had been spent staring at the same sealed envelope with the letters CDMA stamped in the upper left corner in bold face lettering. Eddy was not yet certain if he wanted to open it. The envelope had been hand delivered by an extremely hairy man right before he had gone home, and he already knew what was inside.

As he sat there, almost entranced by the envelope, he became aware of a faint clicking and buzzing sound over his right shoulder, like the sound of a beetle flying nearby. "Hey Sara" Eddy said without ever looking.

"What is with the envelope?" Sara asked.

"It is my CDMA license" he told her.

"Your kidding!" she chirped excitedly. "They gave you an actual license? You must be the first human in history to ever get one. How did this happen?"

"I am the first" Eddy said numbly. "The Seelie Court, well Max anyways, thought I should have one. She is right. I should. If I am going to be working cases that deal with magic, I need to have full access to the resources to handle them. And I am going to be dealing with magic rather I like it or not."

"Woe, hold on a moment. Back up" Sara said. "Max, as in Maxine Song of the Seelie Court had you deputized?" Eddy nodded. "Wow. That's . . . Wow. I can't think of the last time a Seelie recruited some one directly. And you were recruited by Maxine of all people. The head of the Seelie Court, and she doesn't trust people easily. You must have really made an impression."

"I suppose I did" Eddy said numbly, unable to show any real excitement about it at all.

Sara flew around to hover a couple of feet in front of Eddy, having learned to respect his personal space over the last few months. "Tell me Eddy, if you could go back in time and change things? If you could make it so you never had taken that walk that night. Had never had the vale lifted? If you could erase the last few months, would you?"

Eddy finally took his eyes off of the envelope and looked at the small woman with the stark black hair in the red dress that was hovering in front of him. "No. No I wouldn't. Yes a lot of bad things have happened to me as a result. I mean how many times has some one, or something, tried to kill me?"

"Dose the octopus count?" Sara asked.

Eddy shook his head. "I don't think it was ever after me to be honest. It just wanted the guys in the truck."

"Then four. So that comes out to about once a month. Ruffly any ways" Sara chimed.

Eddy laughed "that was a rhetorical question by the way. What I was going to say, was that a lot of good has come with it. More then the bad. I never would have met you for a start." Sara smiled proudly "or Thena."

"Or Miss Vallen" Sara said.

"Technically, I already knew her" Eddy pointed out.

"Yes, but you didn't know what she was" Sara said enthusiastically.

"Yes. An energy ball throwing bounty hunter. Still not sure what I think of that one to be honest" Eddy said.

"Or Edith" Sara added.

Eddy's smile broadened "or Edith" he agreed. "Speaking of Edith, what do you think of going to stay with her for a while?"

"Are you trying to get rid of me?" Sara said, sounding more then just a little hurt. "It's because of that Rose lady. Because she doesn't like me, isn't it?"

"No. It has nothing to do with Rose" Eddy assured her. "I am just worried about Edith. Things seem to be heating up again, and I am worried that they might go after her."

"They probably don't even know about Edith" Sara said.

"That's what Max said" Eddy told her.

"You see nothing to worry about. Besides if there are bad people after you, shouldn't you be more worried about your own safety?" Sara asked.

"I will be fine. After all, I handled Swan just fine didn't I?" Eddy asked her.

"Handled? Yes. Defeated? No. That would be Edith" Sara pointed out.

"True" Eddy agreed a little shyly.

"She rescued you. He was trying to kill you, and she took him down. She pulled the air right out of his lungs" Sara continued.

Eddy sighed "I get it Sara. What is your point?"

"My point, as you put it, is that she doesn't need looking after. You do" Sara said.

"Please can you just watch after her" Eddy pleaded. "Just help give me a little peace of mind."

"How about this" Sara said. "During the day I will keep an eye on her. After all you have that Carl fellow to keep you out of trouble at work. Then in the evening I will come back here. Will that work for you?"

Eddy smiled "yes, that works for me."

"Good, because it is the only offer you were going to get." Sara smiled. "Now are you going to open that envelope already, or are you waiting for the glue to decompose and let the envelope open on its own?"

"Ok, ok. I will open it." Eddy stuck his finger under the lip on the edge of the envelope, and used his finger like a crude letter opener and tore it open. He then pulled out a letter, and the small plastic card with a picture of his face on it, with the letters CDMA printed next to it in bold print letters. He set the envelope and letter down, and then began staring at the card.

"You are hopeless" Sara said as she gave up and she fluttered over to the potted plant by the window where she would often spend the night.

Chapter 11

A Blue Elf on a Blue Moon

Eddy was once again out for one of his evening walks. Sara had warned him many times on previous occasions that it might not be the wisest of ideas, given that he had managed to attract the attention of a crime syndicate. She had finally conceded to let him go one night after he had promised to take his sword with him. Now that he thought about it, he realized Sara had not come back home from Edith's tonight. He would have to call Edith in the morning to see what was going on. He reassured himself with the thought that the night had simply gotten cold to fast for Sara, and that she had probably decided to spend the night there.

Eddy enjoyed his walks. Late at night the city became quieter. Never completely devoid of sound, but quiet enough that when one walked along the river like he was now, one could almost forget that they were surrounded by man made canyons and spires of concrete and glass.

Sense gaining the sight at the end of the summer, Eddy had found that he enjoyed his walks even more then he had before. He had discovered that many creatures wondered the city at night. Over time he had become friends with some of them. As he passed under a familiar overpass he found himself coming up on the home of one of them.

Eddy pulled the collar of his coat closer around his neck to try and keep out the cold. He may like his nightly walks, but he hated the cold of winter. As he made his way across the dead frozen plants and walked up to the ice caked brown cattail stalks sticking out of the unfrozen water, he wondered about if his dislike for the cold had anything to do with his element being fire. He began to hear a light giggling over the crunching of his footsteps in the hard snow. He then came to a stop as a pair of gray eyes with gold speckling appeared in the water before him.

"Hello Eddy" came the childlike voice from the water. "How are you?"

Eddy knelled down next to the water "I am good" he said. "A little cold, but good. How are you tonight?" The water bubbled up to form a spire, it then took on the shape of a small child in a white dress. The little girl wore a string of fresh water clam shells dangling from fishing line around her neck.

"What's cold like? I don't get cold" Cindy told him.

Eddy smiled at the nymph. Though Eddy had learned that she was old enough to be his mother she still looked, and acted like a child. "Cindy I don't think I can explain that one." Cindy often asked Eddy questions about being human. Eddy was after all the only human that she had ever talked to, which meant there was a lot she did not know about them.

Cindy smiled briefly, but then sighed. "I miss my frog" she said.

"What happened to your frog?" Eddy asked sympathetically. "Did it die?"

The small girl giggled like the five year old she looked like. "No silly. He is sleeping. Hibernating. That's what humans call it, right? But he will be back. When the frosts stop coming that is."

Eddy gazed down the long length of the river as it rippled past them. "I have often wondered why the river never freezes over. Never completely any ways."

"Oh that is easy" the nymph said with pride. "Magic! Many rivers won't ice over because of magic. A long time ago dragons put spells on the rivers that they called their homes. Most of the dragons are gone now, but their magic is still around. Magic that strong last a really long time."

"Oh" Eddy said simply. After the last several months things did not surprise him as much as they once had.

Cindy stood bare foot on the bank twirling her dress back and forth clearly proud that she had taught Eddy something. The white dress sparkled like snow, just as it had been every night sense the first frost, but tonight it looked slightly different. It looked a light blue.

"So dose your dress change color with the season?" Eddy asked curiously. In the months sense he had first met Cindy her dress had always been white, that is until tonight.

"Oh that would be neat, but no its white as always" she said giggling. "It only looks blue because of the moon. It is after all, a blue moon."

Eddy was well aware that it was the second full moon this month, often referred to as a blue moon. He however did not know what that had to do with her dress. That is until he looked up at the moon itself. The moon was in fact a vivid blue. The color of blue like he had seen in pictures of icebergs.

Eddy stood up in awe. "Well I'll be. So that is where it gets the name. You know Cindy, if you can't see through the veil, a blue moon looks just like any other full moon."

Eddy looked down at Cindy smiling, but the smile quickly left his face. Cindy looked nervous. "Someone is coming" she whispered.

"Are they human?" Eddy asked her. Cindy just shook her head. "Can you tell what they are?" he asked.

"No" the girl said, sounding more then just a little scared. "I've never felt any thing like it before, but it is old. Really old."

Cindy looked up at him wide eyed, and then froze. Eddy waited for her to say something, and then realized the nymph was in fact, frozen.

"Cindy!" Eddy yelled at the frozen girl. He reached out to touch her, and the cold made his hands ache, even through his glove.

"Forget about your little nymph friend. She will be fine" said a female voice from behind him. "Calling me old. The nerve, really. Do I look old to you?"

Eddy turned around to find a tall slender young woman in a sleek silver gown standing behind him. Her eyes were the same icy color as the blue moon, and she had long pointed ears running back along the sides of her head. All the features of her face and skin were completely smooth, as if they had been carved out of marble. Her skin was the same color of blue as a robin's egg. There was no question in Eddy's mind, that this had to be a blue elf.

"Your friend is merely frozen. She will be fine once she thaws. I wanted to talk to you alone" the woman said to him. "I would have stopped by your home, but I can not seem to find it. It's as if your apartment simply dose not exist anymore. I take it that it must be under some sort of glamour spell. But that is ok, this works just as well, and much easier then breaking the blasted spell."

"If you froze Cindy, then I take it you are the one that has been creating the creatures made of ice that I have been running into?" Eddy asked her nervously.

"No, that's not me. One of my associates handled that. Such an artiest she is. You should really appreciate it more" the blue elf told him.

"Maybe when one of them is not trying to kill me" Eddy said.

The tall woman chuckled lightly and smiled at him. "Don't be so defensive. I am not here to hurt you. To be honest Detective we haven't meant you any real harm. You see, we believe you simply have something that belongs to me. My name is Cecelia by the way, but you probably already figured that one out, but back to the subject at hand. When you arrested pore little Ezekiel over the summer, we believe he was in possession of something of mine. A trinket really, but mine none the less, and I want it back."

"I honestly don't know. I wasn't the one that processed him" Eddy told her.

"Oh Eddy don't lie to me. I know you were there." Cecelia paused briefly, as if in thought. "To think pore Ezekiel was beaten up by this mere human. It stands beyond reason as a possibility" she said, more to herself then to Eddy. He tried to interrupt her, but she cut him off before he could. "I have no doubt there is more to you then we know" this time, she was talking to him "so we have been watching you. I expect you to get my little trinket, and return it to me."

"I don't have it" Eddy said before she could cut him off again. "I don't' even know what you are talking about."

"Maybe not, but your little CD, whatever it is, does" she said, clearly irritated.

"I can't just go and take a prisoners personal possessions" Eddy told her.

"MY possession! Not his." Cecelia was clearly getting angry.

"Then simply go down and claim it" Eddy said as he considered pulling the sword from his inside pocket.

Cecelia just chuckled darkly. "Someone like me does not just walk into a Seelie Court facility." She stepped closer to Eddy and starred him in the eye's "and don't even think about trying to poke me with that little toy of yours. You would be dead before you drew it from your pocket, let alone transformed it into anything of use." The tall woman smiled pleasantly at Eddy. She then reached out and straightened the collar of Eddy's coat, and smoothed the wrinkles out of his sleeves.

"You are clearly a clever young man. I have no doubt you will find a way to get it for me." Then the wind suddenly picked up and the woman dissolved into it right before Eddy's eyes.

Eddy blinked as the wind subsided, then quickly pulled out his cell phone and began to dial.

"Hello?" croaked Carl's groggy voice over the phone.

"Hey Carl. Sorry to wake you, but we have a problem" Eddy said.

Chapter 12

Evidence Room

It was another late night, and Carl and Eddy were back at the CDMA Central Annex. This time around the guardian had given Eddy no trouble as he had climbed the steps to enter the capital, having apparently excepted his presence. The only reaction it had given was a slight nod as he passed over the large brick compass shaped courtyard that the statue rested in. They had not come to see the Seelie, nor had they come to talk to Swan again, even thought Eddy found he really wanted to. He had some more questions for the man, and he wanted answers to them. He would have set up an appointment himself, except for the fact that he had no idea how to do it, nor did he know the password to get by the sliding door. Thinking about it now, he figured he probably should find out now that he had a CDMA license. It would be impractical to have to call Carl every time he needed to come to the annex, however often that would be.

This time around however they had come to visit a rather bland room. The room consisted of not much more then the four concrete walls that formed its non exiting uniformly square shape. The room was lined with row upon row of identical wooden shelves. In truth it looked in general just like any other police evidence room, with the exception that part of its contents looked like it either belonged in an antique shop or a props department. Eddy glanced over at Carl as he stood nearby meticulously flipping through the pages of an enormous inventory log. Eddy turned his attention back to the shelf in front of him, as a fish head floating in a jar filled with a honey colored fluid turned and looked at him.

Eddy reached up to tap the side of the glass jar when Carl called out to him. "I would not do that if I were you. Those things get angry easily, and that glass looks way thinner then it should be to hold something like that."

"What is it exactly?" Eddy asked as he took a few steps back to increase the distance between himself and the jar.

"Probably best that I don't tell you. It might just give you nightmares" Carl told him as he walked past. "Come on. I found it."

Eddy glanced back at the now grinning contents of the jar before he hurriedly fallowed after the giant. "And what is it you found exactly?"

"Another lead" Carl called back. "I realized that there was a good chance that someone in the CDMA may have looked into Summer's death. After all, lightning strikes on a clear night, beneath bridges, is not exactly an everyday event."

"That is what I told people. Look where that got me" Eddy said.

"It got you the truth, if I am not mistaken" Carl pointed out. "Anyways, it turns out someone had looked into it. Scott Peyo to be exact."

"Who?" Eddy interrupted.

"Our lightning wielding truck driver that took a dive through a window" Carl informed him.

"Oh" Eddy answered as he looked briefly down at the floor. "How is he doing by the way?"

"Oh, he will be fine. It will take more then that to put him out of commission. In fact he will be back on the streets before the next full moon. Anyways, it turns out Summers had more then his keys and an ID on him that night. He has a small stone figure on him as well."

Eddy looked over at Carl with a faint smile as he caught up to him. "You mean like an artifact?"

"Exactly" Carl said as he came to a stop in front of one of the shelves and picked up a Ziploc bag with a foreign drivers license, set of keys, two sticks of gum and a three inch tall gray stone statue inside of it.

The Statue, in general, was rather unimpressive. Carved of some unknown, plain gray stone, it was almost completely lacking of any real detail. The features were rounded like that of a balloon. Its arms were sticking straight out to the sides and its legs hung straight down, making it stand in the position rather like that of a scarecrow. That is if it could stand on its stubby rounded footless legs. The small person looked more like something a preschooler would make from clay at daycare rather then an item that someone would be killed for.

The only thing that stood out at all about the figure was its face, or more accurately were the face should be. The entire front of the head consisted of a single, enormous eye. The eye, unlike the rest of the figures features was extremely detailed. As Eddy looked at it he half expected it to blink.

"So that's is it?" Eddy asked, not able to take his gaze off of the statues eye like head.

"Yep. The thing that Travis supposedly lost, and Cecelia thinks Ezekiel recovered before his arrest" Carl told him.

"But what is it? Other then ugly that is?" Eddy asked, and Carl chuckled. "And why does Cecelia want it bad enough to kill for it?" he said, his smile leaving his face.

"I wish I knew" Carl answered. "The more I learn, the more things I realize I don't know. We keep finding more questions then answers." Carl opened the bag and pulled out the little stone man. "Like why was Swan sent to kill a man for loosing something that the man had in his pocket?"

"Maybe Summers told them he lost it?" Eddy suggested.

"But why? Why would he take that risk? He had to of known they would come after him" Carl asked.

"Maybe" Eddy began "Maybe he felt it was worth it. Maybe he felt this thing was worth more then his life. What if what they want it for is so big, that he was willing to die to prevent it?"

"In which case, it must be magical" Carl stated.

"But what dose it do?" Eddy asked.

"I have no idea" Carl looked from the statue to Eddy a little uneasily, "but I think I might know of someone that can tell us."

"Who?" Eddy asked him.

"You probably won't like this" Carl said "but your friend Edith."

"Edith!" Eddy said in shock. "What on earth makes you think she would know anything about it?"

"Well magical objects seems to be something she knows a lot about. Charms anyways" Carl told him. "If it is some kind of charm, which I think it probably is, maybe she can tell us what it dose. If we know what it dose, we can figure out what they want it for."

"What do you mean she is good with charms?" Eddy asked him.

Carl pointed at the slight bump beneath Eddy's shirt, and said "she made that didn't she?" Eddy looked down at his hand as he placed it gently over the velvety pouch that hung around his neck hidden underneath his shirt. Edith had given it to him over the summer, and the magic inside of it had saved his life. "There is some potent magic in that thing. If there wasn't you would most definitely be dead. You took multiple lighting strikes at close range, to the chest no less. You survived being mauled by a ice lion. Ether one of those thing would have killed anyone else. So either you are secretly immortal, or it is those charms. Personally my money is on the charms. You smell too human to be immortal. Which leaves the charms. Meaning that the woman knows her stuff. I want you to take the statue to her and see if she can tell us anything about it."

Carl handed the statue to Eddy, who reluctantly accepted it. It was surprisingly heavy for something so small, and slightly warm to the touch. Eddy gingerly put it in his pocket. "I will take it over to her tomorrow afternoon. She should be home from work by four."

"What is it she dose any ways?" Carl asked him as the two of them began to make their way back through the maze of wooden shelves.

"To be honest, I have no idea" Eddy told him.

Chapter 13

Winston

Eddy hurried home with the statue securely in his inside coat pocket. He pulled over and parked his car on the side of the road a bit farther away from his building then he would have preferred, but this late at night all the closer spots had long sense been taken. The statue seemed to bounce noisily against the antique butter knife that he had tucked away in the same pocket with every step he took. Eddy quickly walked to the door of his apartment building. Carrying something that he knew people were willing to kill for made him more then a little nervous as he made his way through the dark. As alert as he tried to be he was still surprised when a slender man stepped out from the shadows near his building.

"Evening" the man said. "Or morning rather, I suppose, if you want to be technical. How are we today Eddy?"

Eddy eyed the man suspiciously. He wore a long unbuttoned brown duster and a very loose fitting shirt that looked like it was at least three sizes to big for him. "Do I know you?"

The man smiled "oh sorry. I'm Winston" he said as he held out his hand to shake Eddy's. "The court sent me."

Eddy's tension eased and he relaxed at the mention of the Seelie Court. "Oh that is who you are. Sorry thought you were here to hurt me. Given the week I have had I am sure you can understand?"

"Oh of course. If I was you, I'd probably be jumping at every little movement from the shadows and little creek in the wall" Winston said with a chuckle. "I've been sent to pick up the idol."

"Idol?" Eddy asked. "What idol?"

"The little statue thing" Winston said while holding his thumb and fore finger apart to show its height.

"Oh!" Eddy exclaimed. "The ugly little statue."

Winston nodded enthusiastically. "So you do have it? Awesome!" the eager man held out his hands just like a kid expecting a prize. "Go ahead and give it to me."

"But Carl asked me to have it identified" Eddy protested.

"Carl? Who is . . . Never mind. We don't need it identified, we already know what it is" Winston told him.

"You do? How? How does the Seelie Court even know about it. I just found out an hour ago." Eddy started to back up.

"Seelie Court? I'm-"

"Winston Carter? Is that you?" called a familiar woman's voice.

Winston's eyes grew big and he slowly turned around to look down the street behind him. "Tabatha Vallen? I thought you were dead" he said with shock.

Mrs. Vallen walked down the street with China, her spiny little pet chupacabra lizard on its leash. "And I'm surprised you are not" she said to the young man with a smile.

Eddy looked at the troll as she walked towards them, a leash in one hand and her long green fingers of her other hand warped around her gnarled wooden cane. "You two know each other?" he asked in disbelief.

"You could say that" Mrs. Vallen told him. "It has been a long time sense I last saw Winston here. Stealing purses and potion ingredients, if I recall" she said to the young man.

"I've moved up in the world Tabatha" Winston said with pride.

"I am glad to hear it, I think. So what brings you to this neck of the woods?" Mrs. Vallen asked him.

Winston looked up and down the street at the sparsely planted trees growing through their round iron drain grates. "Think it takes more trees then this to count as the woods."

Mrs. Vallen smiled and shook her head "same old Winston. I mean why are you here boy?"

"The court sent him to pick up something from me" Eddy told her. "You never told me, how dose the Seelie already know about it anyways? I haven't even called Max yet. I was waiting to have something to tell her first."

Winston smiled a little. "No, no, no. Not the Seelie, the other one."

Eddy took a few more steps away, and Winston frowned. "Mrs. Vallen" Eddy called to the old woman. "I don't think you should be proud of what he considers moving up."

Mrs' Vallen sighed "I was afraid of that."

Winston slid the long coat off of his shoulders and let it fall noisily to the frost covered sidewalk. "I really didn't want to do it this way" the man said with almost a growl. He bent over slightly and curled his arms inward, just like a body builder flexing his muscles.

Indeed the muscles did expand, but much larger then one would have expected. His arms grew to almost fill the extremely baggy shirt sleeves with the now bulging muscles. As his muscles grew the man also grew slightly taller, and his knees bent backwards with a loud pop.

The sound made Eddy look down for the first time, and that is when he noticed the man was only waring sandals, despite the cold. As he looked the man's toes grew and curled out past the end as his long claw like nails clicked on the ground. Eddy's head snapped up as a beastly snarl tore through the still air. Winston's now massive face was covered in dark thick hair, every square inch of it, down to the end of his long dog like snout. Eddy was no expert on super natural beings, but there was no doubt in his mind what he was looking at. The things were renowned in books and movies. Winston was a werewolf.

Eddy stepped backward and a long toothy grin appeared on the wolfs face. "So it's true you can see us for what we really are. Cooool" Winston said in his now much lower gravely voice.

Eddy pulled the small butter knife from his pocket and it quickly transformed it into a long silvery sword. Eddy drew the sword back, poised to strike as he watched the man's massive clawed fingers flex and unflex.

"Nice sword" Winston admired. "They didn't say you knew any magic."

"Not high enough up the totem pole to get all the details are we?" asked Eddy.

Winston studied Eddy as he tried to decide how to proceed. "To be honest I don't think they knew. But that's ok. New information is always appreciated."

"Then lets make it worth while." Eddy briefly closed his eyes, and the blade of the sword coated itself in an amber colored flames. *At least I can light the sword. But of course it is a part of the sword. Being excited about turning on its flame is like being excited about turning on a flashlight. It is what it was made to do, but turning this light on just might be able to save his life* he thought.

Winston stepped back, now a lot less certain then he had been a moment ago. The wolf man studied Eddy for a while, pacing slightly as he watched him. Then he suddenly jumped into the air and came right down on top of Eddy.

Eddy swung the sword towards the descending werewolf and caught him in the arm where his sword was met with a loud metallic clank. The force knocked Eddy to the ground, and as he looked up he saw that the man's watch had expanded into a metal gauntlet that now ran more then halfway up his massive hairy arm.

"I have my tricks to" Winston said with a grin.

Eddy gasped for air. He had landed hard on his back, and the force had knocked the wind out of him. Trying to take in the frigged air burned, but he needed to get up and forced the air into his lungs anyways. "I see that" Eddy wheezed as he got back up off of the ground. Eddy lifted his sword and held it at the ready as he looked the wolf man in his copper colored eyes. "So isn't there some stupid question that you want to ask me? You know, the kind with an obvious answer?"

Winston shook his shaggy head. "No. Why would I?"

"I don't know. It's just something everyone in the last few months that has tried to kill me has done" Eddy told him.

"Really?" Winston said as he paced back and forth and tried to decide his next move. "Like what?"

"Things like, is it ok if I kill you?" Eddy told him. "You know, stupid questions of like that."

Winston snickered, which sounded odd coming from a giant up right wolf. "That is a stupid question. Who in their right mind would say yes to a question like that? But no, I'm no going to ask you some stupid question like that. After all, I'm not here to kill you. I just want the idol. Then we can all walk away happy."

"So what is it for anyways?" Eddy asked him, keeping his sword up and ready to fend off the were.

Winston smiled "if you don't know, I am not going to tell you. I'm young, not stupid."

"So you don't know? Is that what you mean?" Eddy said while never taking his eyes off of the pacing werewolf.

"I'm not falling for it Eddy" Winston told him, and then suddenly he dashed forward and slammed his full body weight into Eddy's shoulder and knocked him off balance. Then before Eddy could regain his footing, Winston slipped behind him with lighting speed and grabbed hold of his collar and hoisted him off of the ground. Eddy attempted to swing his sword, but could not get his arm far enough behind him and ended up dropping it instead. "It's in your coat pocket isn't it? I can smell its magic" he said as he leaned his large head closer to Eddy and inhaled.

Winston began to reach for Eddy's inside pocket when suddenly a bright flash lit up the backside of the wear's head. He dropped Eddy and howled in pain. Winston started to turn around just when another bright flash hit him hard in the side of his face. Eddy could clearly see that the wolf man's head was now on fire. The purple glow bathing the street in a faint light and filled it with the putrid smell of burnt hair and skin. Winston dropped down on all fours and sprinted down the street leaving rancid tendrils of smoke in his wake.

"Well that was a close one" said Mrs Vallen. Eddy looked up as he once again pulled himself up off of the ground. Eddy was also once again glade to see the old green troll standing there. She had saved him again. "You know my boy, I think we need to have another one of our talks, don't you."

Chapter 14

History

Eddy fell in line next to Mrs Vallen as they walked to their apartment building. They walked quietly at first, that is until Eddy suddenly broke the silence.

"You set him on fire!" Eddy finally blurted out.

"Yes I set him on fire" Mrs Vallen said solemnly. "Believe me Eddy, I take no joy in injuring the poor boy. I just hope I did not burn him to badly. Winston is not a bad kid. He just has a habit of getting involved with the wrong people."

They walked in silence for a moment before Eddy spoke again. "Why didn't you step in to help me sooner?" he asked her.

"You didn't seem to need my help, but you had clearly lost your advantage, and Winston was about to get what ever it was he was after" she told him. Eddy began to speak, but Mrs Vallen cut him off before he could utter his first word. "I think it is best if we save the rest of our conversation for more privet quarters. Say your apartment. I would normally prefer my own, but given that a few months back your door vanished, I suspect your place might be a better choice."

"Oh, my door" Eddy began "that's because-"

"Indoor conversation" Mrs Vallen told him as they climbed the salt incrusted stairs and entered the old brick apartment building.

They climbed the stairs to their floor and up to where Eddy's door should be. As soon as Eddy touched the key to the wall where the lock would be, the door magically appeared. Eddy fumbled with the lock to his door for some time before the key slide into the hole and he finally heard the click of the lock disengaging. He opened the door and began to walk inside, then stopped and stepped back out. He then moved to the side and motioned for Mrs Vallen to go in first. The old women smiled sweetly at the fumbling detective as she passed by him to enter the apartment.

As Eddy closed the door he found Mrs Vallen standing nearby, looking at the mirror on the wall next to his door. "So that is why your door has disappeared" she said.

"It is a glamour spell" Eddy told her as he closed the door

"You don't need to tell me what it is" Mrs Vallen said. "I am well aware. But how on earth did you come by one?"

"Edith made it for me" Eddy told her.

"Well consider me impressed" Mrs Vallen said as she turned and walked over and took a seat on the only thing to sit on in Eddy's living room, his couch.

"So how do you know Winston?" Eddy asked her as he walked over to join her. He stood for a moment before taking an uncomfortable seat next to her on the couch.

"I arrested him more then once when he was a teen" she told him. "Never for anything major mind you. It was always small things. Bits and pieces of trivialities here and there, but it was enough to get attention. He is not a bad kid, he just gets wrapped up in bad things. I personally tried on multiple occasions to help him reform. It would appear I failed." Mrs Vallen turned to look at him. "Now this time you are the one that needs to do some explaining. What was this nonsense Winston was saying about the UnSeelie Court?"

Eddy looked at the troll uneasily. Mrs Vallen in turn looked at him patiently awaiting an answer. "It's not nonsense" Eddy finally said. "He is working for the UnSeelie"

"That's impossible" Mrs Vallen insisted. "The UnSeelie no longer exist."

"I am afraid they do" Eddy told her. "Apparently they have just been laying low."

"Laying low, sense the end of the Renaissance?" said Mrs Vallen in disbelief. "Now that is what I call patients."

"Well apparently the blue elves have run out of patients, and decided to become active again" he said.

"Blue elves!" Mrs Vallen exclaimed. "First you tell me that the UnSeelie Court is not only still around, but active. Now you are telling me that they are connected to an extinct race, that is apparently not extinct after all?"

"Yes" Eddy said.

Mrs Vallen shook her head. "Eddy, if I didn't know any better I would say you were spinning fairy tails." The elderly troll took a deep breath. "Eddy I think you better start at the beginning. The very beginning."

"Then we will have to go back to the end of summer" Eddy told her. "That is when I witnessed a man's murder. He was killed by lighting on a clear night. In the process of trying to find his killer, Xander felt it was best to lift the vale so I could see things for what they really are. Remember that day I freaked out in the hall?"

Mrs Vallen smiled "I remember it well."

Eddy looked at the floor shyly, now realizing how ridicules he must have looked that day. "Any ways, as time went by I eventually learned that he was killed by a whit named Ezekiel Swan."

"You were trying to track down a whit!" Mrs Vallen shouted at him.

"Found him to. More by chance then skill, I am sorry to say" Eddy told her.

"How on earth did you survive?" she asked him.

Eddy pulled the small pouch out of his shirt and stared at it. "Edith" he said. "She made the charms in this bag. Without it, his lighting would have killed me. She also trained me how to use a sword, and tried to teach me magic so I could stand a chance against him."

"You defeated him?" she asked, entranced by his story.

"No" he said. "Edith did. She used her powers to pull the air out of his lungs."

"Smart girl" Mrs Vallen said with a smile.

"That she is" Eddy agreed, and Mrs Vallen's smile broadened.

"Now just to clarify" Mrs Vallen said. "Edith is the pretty brunette with the unbelievably long hair, right?"

"Yes, that would be her" Eddy said. Mrs Vallen smiled. "A short while back Carl learned why Swan had killed the man."

"Carl?" Mrs Vallen asked.

"He would be my giant new partner" Eddy said. "I've know him for a while, just did not know he was a giant until he showed up to cuff Swan. We just recently became partners. Turns out the man I had seen killed, had supposedly lost some little idol, and Swan killed him for it. Thing is, he had not really lost it after all. He lied. The idol was on him when he died, but sense I was there when Swan killed him, he never had a chance to check. Honestly I don't think Swan was even planing to."

"So what does this all have to do with the UnSeelie Court?" Mrs Vallen asked him.

"That would be who they all worked for. They are members of the UnSeelie Court" Eddy told her.

"But what do they want some idol for?" she asked him.

"I don't know" Eddy said. "I was going to take it over to Edith's tomorrow and see what she could tell me about it. But maybe you could save me a trip." Eddy said as he began to reach into his coat pocket.

"Sorry Eddy. Idols and charms are really not my thing. Not like my nephew, he could tell you" Mrs Vallen said. "I am afraid I wont be of any help to you however. I can activate things, but that is the extent of my knowledge on charms. Speaking of which, your sword. When did you get that?"

"End of the summer. Shorty after the wraiths" Eddy said.

"And you can light it on fire" she said with a hint of admiration. "A human that can work magic. It's incredible."

"Less incredible then it seems. The fire is a part of the sword" Eddy told her. "All I do is invoke it. I can use fire, but can't get it to work for me."

"Then how do you know you can use fire?" she asked.

"I lit a piece of metal on fire when I was fighting against Swan" Eddy explained.

"Did you?" Mrs Vallen said intrigued. "How did that come about? The fire, not the fight."

"He was going to kill Edith, Xander and their friend, Crystal. I had to do something" Eddy said.

"But it has not happened sense?" she asked. Eddy just shook his head. "Curiosity, what were you thinking at the time?"

"I don't know" Eddy said. "It all happened so fast. I just remember that . . . I had to protect them. They are to important to me. I could not let any thing happen to her."

"Have you thought about that night when you are trying to invoke your power?" Mrs Vallen asked him.

"Often" he told her. "I think about it all the time. It doesn't work."

Mrs Vallen smiled "maybe my boy, you are thinking about the wrong thing. I suspect there was more going through your heart that night then just the desire to protect your friends." Her smile broadened. "But you are a bright boy. I have no doubt you will figure it out before long."

The elderly trolls smile faded. "Eddy. I've told you this before. Be careful. I have never dealt with the UnSeelie Court. They predate me, or, so I thought. But I do know they are bad news. It probably goes without saying, but you need to watch yourself." She got up and began to walk to the door. "Keep yourself safe." She opened the door to leave, then turned around to look at Eddy one more time. "And protect those you care about, once they're gone they're gone for good." She then closed the door and was gone. Leaving Eddy alone to think about what she had said.

Chapter 15

The Storm Before the Calamity

It was getting late, and Eddy was finally leaving the station. Ever sense he had become an official member of the CDMA he had found himself working longer hours. It was not that he had more cases, it was primarily do to having to take care of all the extra paper work. One set for the Denver Police, and another set containing what really happened for the CDMA. As soon as Eddy stepped out of the door he suddenly found Carl walking beside him.

"Hey Eddy" Carl said with an uneasy smile.

"Hi Carl" Eddy said.

"So" the large man continued "you are going to go see your friend Edith today?" Eddy nodded. "Mind if I . . . um . . . tag along?"

Eddy stopped in his tracks and looked at Carl "You want to come with me? Why?"

Carl started walking towards the parking lot again and Eddy fallowed. "To be honest I am a little worried about you. In less then a twelve hour period two members of the UnSeelie Court made direct contact with you. One of which was their leader no less." Carl began to look around him "where is your sprite escort by the way?"

"Sara?" Eddy asked. "To be honest, I don't know. She hasn't come back from Edith's for two days now. I tried to call this morning, but Edith won't pick up her phone. Honestly I am getting more then a little worried about her."

"Then I am defiantly coming with you" Carl said assertively.

"I take it that means we will be taking your car?" Eddy said as the first few flakes of a light snow begun to fall.

"It is roomier" Carl said shyly.

"Uh huh" was all Eddy could say without smiling. As they climbed into Carl's station wagon the snow continued to gain in momentum.

"Wow, it is really starting to come down" Eddy said as he leaned foreword to stare out the windshield.

"No kidding" Carl agree. "This could turn into quite the little adventurer if it decides to stick to the roads" Carl said as he put the car into gear and drove out of the parking lot. As they drove the snow began falling so fast that Carl had to turn on the windshield wipers before they had even made it a block from the station. They slowly made their way down the desolate streets of Denver. This late at night on a weekday traffic was normally fairly light, but the rapid dropping temperatures, combined with the increasing snow, had turned this part of the city into a virtual ghost town. Well a brightly lit ghost town anyways. The streetlights shined brightly in the night as they illuminated every snow flake in the vicinity as they drifted through the air glowing like tiny little cinders.

Suddenly a dark object darted in front of the car and Carl had to slam on his brakes to avoid hitting it. The station wagon fishtailed, and slid on the ice before it finally came to rest against a light poll with a loud crash.

Carl's knuckles were white from gripping the steering wheel. "You all right Eddy?" he asked with out ever taking his eyes off of the light poll in front of him.

"Yeah I'm fine" Eddy told him. "What was that?"

"I think it was a person. Blasted idiot. There are crosswalks for a reason!" he yelled at the closed drivers side window. "At least I didn't hit them" he said, sounding a bit more reserved. Carl released the steering wheel, flexed his fingers, and then unbuckled his seat belt and opened the car door. "Well I guess I better get out and see how bad the damage is."

Carl walked around to the front of the car, and immediately began to frown at the large vertical dent that now ran through the center of his front bumper. Frustrated, he kicked at the front of the car which only resulted in yet another large dent. Carl frowned at the newest dent, and then began to shake his head wearily.

"Well, I suppose we should see if I can get the car backed off of this poll so we can get back under way" Carl said drearily.

Eddy nodded as he looked down the vacant street wondering were the person who had run in front of them had gone.

"I'm afraid I can not allow that" came a woman's voice from behind them.

Carl and Eddy spun around to see a woman standing behind them. She had ruddy colored skin, and jet black hair that hung loosely around her shoulders. Despite the cold, the woman was dressed in a tank top and running shorts looking more like she should be running track rather then taking a stroll in a snow storm. Despite the woman's unseasonal attire something else drew Eddy's attention. Coming out from the sides of the woman's head, just above the ears, were a set of large shinny black ram horns that stuck out to the side nearly a foot in length, curling in tight spirals like a pair of corkscrews.

"Who are you?" Eddy asked unable to hide the nervousness from showing in his voice.

The woman smiled, looking pleased by Eddy's question. "A messenger" she said "and if all goes well tonight, a delivery girl. Now hand over the idol Eddy" she said as she held out a hand with long round black nails. "We know you have it. So make things easy. Just hand it over." Eddy slowly reached into his coat, and the woman's smile broadened "that's a good boy Eddy. I really didn't want to hurt you."

Eddy withdrew his hand, and the light shined dimly off of the small object that rested in the palm of his hand. Then suddenly there was a bright flair of light as the street lights reflected off of the long gleaming silver blade of his sword as it appeared. The snow melted quickly as it touched the smooth warm surface of the sword.

"So you want to do it the hard way? Fine!" the demonic looking woman spat. "Always thought you were smarter then this Eddy. But I'll play."

Carl brought out his hammer and stood ready to strike "Stay back Eddy. I'll handle this."

"Oh Carl, you only wish you could" the woman laughed.

Carl glared at the woman "don't let her get close. Do not let her touch you" he warned.

The woman grinned "oh by the way, you probably should have turned your car off."

"And why is that lady" Carl said, not liking the tone in her voice at all.

A shadow began to fall over the two men as the woman stared behind them, the smile never leaving her face. They hesitantly looked over their shoulder and then quickly spun around, turning their backs to the woman entirely. Rising out from the street, as easily as if it were something rising from a pool of water, was a large translucent dome the size of a city bus. The sound of its forming had been completely droned out by the rumbling of Carl's car engine. If he had turned it off they would have heard it, but now it was too late. They were trapped.

A second dome formed in front of the first with eight facets running across the front in a wide "v" shape. As the domes rose they took on a more spherical shape, and branching began to sprout out from the back of the front sphere like eight slender roots running along the ground. As the thing grew the two spheres began to hook together. Suddenly the branches pushed upwards flinging the body into the air as it stood on what where now clearly legs. The beast towered over them. Its massive crystal like body was twice the size of a gray hound bus. Its spider like body shone a bluish tint in the snowy light of the street.

The men began to back down the street when suddenly Carl stopped moving and took on a stance that was a strange combination between ridged and relaxed. When Eddy looked over at him he saw that the woman had grabbed the back of the large mans neck. She smiled, and a look of pleasure crawled across Carl's face.

"Let go of him!" Eddy demanded, swinging the point of the sword towards her.

"And why would I do that?" she said and a wicked smile crawled across her face. "Besides, I think he enjoys it. Don't you Carl?"

"Yeah Eddy" Carl said with a giddy smile. "She doesn't need to let go. Hey I have an idea. Why don't we just give the lovely lady the statue."

"What are you doing to him?" Eddy yelled as he pointed the sword at her more threateningly.

"Making his dreams come true" she said with a sly smile.

"I doubt that lady. Now let him, go!" Eddy screamed at her as Carl's face began to go pail.

Eddy lurched forward, drawing his sword back in order to deliver a killing blow. The woman scowled, then shoved Carl hard at Eddy. He tried to stop his swing, but slipped on the ice, falling to the ground in the process and slid painfully a short distance. Carl laid on the ground near by, face down and limp. Eddy frantically crawled over to him.

Eddy rolled the large man over onto his back, and was relieved to see that he was still breathing. He had a vacant stare, and yet a look of pure euphoria on his face. Suddenly there was a sharp crashing sound nearby. It sounded like the sound of crushing metal. When Eddy turned towards the sound he saw that one of the giant spiders legs had gone right through the hood of Carl's car.

Carl stared at his mangled car and smiled. Then he blinked a few times, and then he screamed "my car! She killed my car!"

He stood up and quickly cupped his hands together, and the area between them began to glow intensely. Carl then suddenly thrust his arms out as he opened his hands, and a blinding ball of light shot out of them and slammed hard into the belly of the beast. The light inside fractured as it made its way back out, and for an instant bathed the street in a series of countless rainbows that sparkled as they reflected off of the ever falling snow.

"Blast it!" Carl said with a scowl. "Blasted things body is like a presume. My magic wont work on it." He looked over at Eddy "yours should though. It's ice. Try and melt it."

Eddy frowned "I told you. I can't get it to work again. I've tried."

Carl lifted up his hammer. "Then I guess we will have to do this the hard way." The end of Carl's hammer began to hum and the surrounding air took on an ozone smell. Carl charged forward and slammed the head of the hammer hard into the nearest leg causing it to crack, but before he could take another swing the spider kicked him away.

Eddy's sword lit up with its familiar amber glow as he ran foreword and swung with the burning blade and cleaved off the end of one of the legs. The enormous spider staggered briefly, but the leg shimmered and replaced itself before Eddy could even attempt to reach the next one.

"NO!" screeched the demonic woman. "Blast you Eddy. You are not supposed to know how to do magic. This is not how all this was supposed to go." She stomped her foot hard and and the spider did the same, piercing Carl through the stomach just below the rib cage.

Eddy's sword spurted, and its flame went out as he ran to Carl. The emotion that was required to light it had been replaced by a new one as he saw his friend laying on the snow covered street.

Eddy knelt beside Carl who was barley breathing. The woman smiled as she walked towards them, clearly satisfied with the outcome.

"Now that is how this is supposed to go" the woman said with a smile.

"I thought you said you didn't want to kill us?" Eddy asked angrily as he checked Carl's slowing pulse.

"No Eddy. I said, I did not want to kill you. I never said anything about him" she said as she continued to canter towards them smiling. "Now give me the statue and we can go home."

Eddy stood up and spun around swinging the sword in a sloppy but vicious arc at the woman as he did so. "Stay away from me" he yelled at her. The woman backed up. "What is so blasted special about this thing that you are so willing to kill people for it?"

"You don't need to know that" the woman said. "There is a lot you didn't need to know. Wouldn't life be simpler if you never knew about any of this? My dear Eddy, just give me the statue, and I can make it all go away."

Eddy stared hard at her, his sword held steady pointed towards her throat. "For some reason I don't think I would like the way you would arrange that."

The woman's smile broadened. "Oh I think you would. Just like Disney Land, except no long lines, or talking animals. Well maybe a few talking animals, if you really want them. You always wanted to go to Disney Land, didn't you Eddy."

"I don't' think so" Eddy said, never lowering the sword.

"But Eddy I am so hungry" the woman said.

The woman smiled, and then the street lights dimmed for a fraction of a second, fallowed immediately by a blindingly bright flash of light that sent the woman whirling backwards threw air. As she hit the ground she slid on the ice for several feet, one of her horns grinding noisily on the frozen asphalt as she went.

Eddy looked to his side to see Carl standing on his knees, his arms outstretched, and a broad grin stretched across his face. The large mans meaty arms sagged to his sides, and he fell over in the snow. The grin never faltered as he laid on the cold ground.

The woman snarled, but Eddy looked at her only briefly as he he ran over and knelt next to Carl and checked his pulse. He no longer had one. The man had used his last breath to protect Eddy, and now he stood alone, pinned between a demon and a monstrous spider made of ice.

The woman lifted herself back up off the street, and brushed the snow off of her self as she spoke. "That is it. I don't care how useful you are. This ends now."

The spider began to sprint forward with a loud clicking sound. Then there began another faint clicking, but this one deeper and faster. Eddy saw a quick flash of motion off to his right, and when he looked a large blue beetle came charging out of a nearby ally. Eddy dove out of the way as it crashed full speed into the legs of the enormous spider, shattering all but one of them. The beast fell to the ground, and the beetle lurched forward and crushed the things head in its massive jaws like a trash compactor crushing a can. Two people dressed as garbage men jumped from behind the head of the beast as it continued to devour the ice monstrosity.

Eddy looked up from the snow as the two men quickly ran over to him. They looked tall, but they might have just looked that way do to with their extremely slender build and disproportionally long arms. The light shined harshly off of what Eddy's originally thought were snow goggles, but as they drew closer he realized they were in fact compound eyes like those of an insect. The two men had faces that reminded Eddy of grasshoppers.

"Are you alright" One of them asked as it held out one of its two fingered armored hands.

Eddy grabbed hold, and was swiftly pulled up from the snow. "Yeah, I am fine."

The one that had helped him out of the snow looked uncomfortably over at Carl's body laying nearby "and, your friend?"

"Carl!" Eddy yelled as he ran back across the snow towards the fallen giant. He fell hard on his knees in the rapidly accumulating snow and instantly started to preform CPR.

The insect men came to stand behind Eddy. One of the bug men removed his knitted stocking cap and brushed back his long antenna, and then placed his hat back on his head as he gave an uneasy look to the man next to him. He placed one of his hands on Eddy shoulder and shook his head "I am so sorry."

Eddy shoved the mans hand away and went back to trying to get Carl's heart pumping again. "Sir there is no point. He is dead" Eddy shook his head, never pausing in trying to revive Carl. "Trust me there is no life left in him." The garbage man lightly grabbed hold of Eddy's arm, and this time, Eddy let him lift him from the snow.

Eddy looked down at Carl's body, then suddenly turned around as he remembered that they were not alone. The demon woman still stood in the center of the street seemingly content to watch events unfold.

Eddy pulled out his gun and pointed it at her, and the woman frowned. "Well this isn't fun any more" she pouted. Suddenly massive leathery wings unfolded as if from no where out of the woman's back, and she took flight. "I'll see you again my dear. Sooner then you think" She blew a kiss at Eddy before she turned and flew off, flying low over a rooftop, snow swirling around her as she went. Eddy considered taking a shot, but lowered his gun as the woman vanished into the swirling snow of the raging storm.

Chapter 16

Edith's

Eddy had ridden along with Carl's body when the ambulance took him to the hospital, where he was officially pronounced dead on arrival. Afterwords Eddy had numbly called for a cab. Only after it had picked him up and dropped him off at his home, did it finally occurred to him that his car was still parked at the police station.

Night had come and gone, and Eddy had suffered through it sleeplessly. With the coming of the morning came determination however. He knew now, more then ever that he had to get to Edith's. People were dieing for this statue, and Eddy needed to know why. If Carl had been right, Edith could tell him more.

Eddy walked over to his phone so that he could call for a cab to take him back to the police station in order pick up his car. Right as he was about to pick up the phone however there came a knock at his door.

"Eddy" came Xander's voice through the door. He sounded uneasy, which was unusual for Xander. Eddy hurried over and opened the door. "I need your help" said Xander before Eddy could even finish opening the door. He stepped into the apartment and almost immediately started pacing around the living room like a person in a hospital waiting room.

"What is wrong?" Eddy asked as he closed the door.

Xander stopped in his tracks and looked hard at Eddy. "It's Edith."

Eddy was suddenly a lot more alert, and worried. "What happened to Edith?"

"Nothing. Well something. I don't know!" Xander tried to explain. "Her work called me this morning. They wanted to know if she was ok.

Apparently she hasn't been to work all this week. You know how she is about missing work. Something is wrong. It has to be."

"To be honest, I think you might be right" Eddy said. "I asked Sara to keep an eye on her during the day, but she hasn't come back to my place in days. I was just about to head over there myself to see what was going on to be honest."

"I'm coming with you" Xander asserted. "I take it we will be taking your car?"

"I, don't have my car right now" he told Xander, who looked at him more then a little confused. "It's still at the police station."

"And why is your car still at work?" Xander questioned.

"It's a long story" Eddy told him solemnly.

Xander started walking to the door, to worried about his sister to be able to tell that something was bothering Eddy. "You can tell me on the way there. Come on, we'll take my car."

*   *   *

Eddy had relayed last nights events to Xander during the car ride, and Xander had listened silently as Eddy told him all about the attack that had led to Carl's death.

"Carl was right" Xander said. "If any one can tell you what that statue they're after is, it is my sister."

"You think so?" Eddy asked quietly.

"I know so. It's her job to know that sort of thing" Xander told him.

Xander put the car in park and quickly jumped out and walked noisily across the dry, frozen grass. There was no sign of snow anywhere, apparently it had failed to do anything more then frost the grass south of Denver. Eddy hurried after him, and just barely got to the door after Xander. The tall man knocked only twice before he produced his own key, and opened the door, not even waiting for some one to answer.

"Hello?" Xander called into the darkened house. "Edith are you here?"

"Edith?" Eddy yelled as well.

They made their way into the house cautiously, looking for any sign that Edith was home. Suddenly they heard a crashing sound come from the basement stairs. Eddy and Xander ran to the staircase, reaching it just as another crash came echoing up from the basement.

Xander ran down the stairs, skipping the last three entirely as he rushed into the basement. Eddy fallowed close behind him. They quickly entered the basements central room. The room was large, nearly the size of the house above. Its wood panel walls were peppered with stacks of boxes, broken only periodically with a few wooden doors. At the far end of the room, at the farthest door, they found Edith standing in front of it holding a crow bar. She had it wedged between the door and its broken frame. Several large pieces of the wooden frame littered the floor, but the door mercilessly appeared untouched.

"Edith what are you doing?" Xander asked in shock.

Edith spun around holding the crow bar defensively. "Nothing" she said quickly, then looked at the crow bar in her hands before she relaxed her grip on it. "Doors stuck" she said nonchalantly. "I must have locked my key inside. Just trying to get it open."

"What do you mean the door is stuck? And what key? Edith that door doesn't lock" Xander said.

Edith punched the door. "Then why won't it open?" she yelled at the door with aggravation, then looked back at Eddy and Xander and tried to relax. "Sorry, just frustrated. What can I do for you two?"

"Eddy wanted you to identify something for him, and I wanted to know why you haven't been to work. They called me this morning, told me you haven't been in all week, and that you haven't been picking up your phone either. What's going on?"

"Haven't been feeling well" Edith said as she walked towards them. "So Eddy why did you want me to see? Another magic marble or something?"

Eddy shook his head. "No, it's a little statue." Eddy reached into his pocket and pulled out the small stone figure, and held it out for her to see. Xander looked down at the statue as Edith's eyes lit up as she stared at it.

"I have never seen anything like it" she said as she reached for the figure.

Suddenly, with out warning, Xander shoved Edith back, causing her to fall backwards, hitting her butt hard on the floor.

"Hey what's the deal?" Eddy yelled at him.

"Yeah what was that for?" Edith complained.

Xander's expression grew dark as he looked at his sister sitting on the floor. "Eddy do not let her touch that thing." He stared hard at Edith "I know what that thing is. That means my sister would know what it is too. You know very well what he is holding, but you are not my sister!"

"Xander what is wrong with you? Did you hit your head or something?" Edith protested. "How could you think I am not your sister?"

"Which of us is older?" Xander demanded.

"Seriously Xander?" Edith whined.

"Answer the question!" the tall man yelled at her.

"You are!" Edith finally blurted, looking like she was going to cry.

Eddy looked over at Xander confused. "Xander, what is going on?"

"As I said, that is not my sister. It's a changeling" Xander said.

The look on Edith's face went from sorrow to anger in an instant. She jumped up from the floor, clutching the crowbar like a club and viciously swung it at them, the tools hooked end just barely missed Eddy's head. Eddy stumbled back, and suddenly Edith dropped the crowbar and ran up the stairs two at at time.

"She has the statue!" Eddy yelled.

The two raced up the stairs after her and reached the top just as she had reached the front door. She looked back as she fumbled to get the door open. She final got it to unlatch, and then quickly flung the door wide, embedding the door knob in the wall, she then promptly ran through the screen door, tarring it clear off its hinges. She stumbled a little as she ran down the front steps and began to cut across the lawn. Eddy and Xander fallowed, close on her heals.

Xander came to a stop suddenly and screamed "STOP!"

Immediately a massive hand made of dirt, clay and rock erupted from the lawn and wrapped itself around Edith. Eddy skidded to a stop, nearly slamming into the earthy fist. Then as quickly as it had appeared, still holding its victim, the hand shot back down into the ground, and vanished, leaving no sign in the lawn that it had ever even existed.

"What was that?" Eddy exclaimed as he stared at the place where the hand had once been mere seconds before.

"Me" Xander stated firmly. "No one messes with my family."

"Did you just kill her?" Eddy asked, still staring at the spot in the lawn.

"No, they're still alive. They're just in the back yard" Xander told him. "Come on, lets go get some answers" he said with finality as he turned around and walked back into the house.

Eddy fallowed Xander as he made his way through the house and into the backyard. Xander stepped out onto the lawn, and the earthy hand slowly rose up out of the yard as clumps of grass clung to the back of it like hair.

"Where is she?" Xander demanded as he stomped across the lawn up to the rising hand.

"I am right here Xander. For crying out loud, let me go" Edith pleaded.

Xander's expression hardened. "Stop lying to me. I know you are not her. What did you do to her? For that mater how did you even find her?" She said nothing, and the fingers of the enormous hand moved inward, closing the fist even more, causing it's prisoner to wheeze. "Where is she!" Xander yelled.

Suddenly Edith's hair began to grow shorter and darker, until it was a shoulder length black tangled mess. Her eyes turned a light orange, and her face grew taller and more slider. Before their eyes the image of Edith continued to transform, until in her place was a raggedy, slender man. Eddy's jaw dropped.

"Tell me where she is" Xander said again.

"Why should I?" The skinny changeling asked.

"Because you want to live" Xander told him.

"You wont kill me" the man said with a smirk.

"And why is that?" Xander asked.

"Because you don't have it in you" the changeling said smugly.

"Oh don't I?" said Xander as the thumb and forefinger of the hand shifted upwards to the man's temples and began to squeeze his head. "You honestly don't think I will kill to protect my family. I will kill you, and anyone that gets in my way in order to get her back."

"But if you kill me, you will never find her" the changeling said as he unsuccessful tried to get his head free from the fingers. "I am your only lead."

Xander walked up until their noses were nearly touching. "That is were you are wrong. I can find her with, or with out your help. Your help just speeds things up a bit."

The confidence on the mans face melted away to fear as he realized that Xander meant every word. "She is in the mountains!" the frightened man said.

"Where in the mountains?" Xander asked him. "The Rockies are a big place. You might want to be a bit more specific".

"I don't know" the man told him. The pressure of the fingers on the mans head began to increase and he began to cry. "I honestly don't know!" he screamed before he began breaking down into deep sobs. The fingers relaxed their grip, and then slide back down around the mans chest.

"I believe you" Xander said, but the man just kept sobbing.

"Now what do we do?" Eddy asked numbly.

"Now? Now we find my sister" Xander told him. As Eddy turned to fallow, he suddenly stopped dead and turned to look back at the man in the yard. "Wait. The statue." The man squirmed a little, and the statue slowly rose out of the the surface of an outstretched finger, and Eddy hesitantly walked up and plucked it out. "What do we do with him?" Eddy asked as he stepped back.

The hand then began to slowly sink back into the ground until it and the man had vanished. "Don't worry, he will be fine" Xander said as he walked onto the porch. "I left him an air shoot. Now come on, lets go get my sister back."

Chapter 17

Maps and Crystals

Eddy fallowed Xander as they walked back into the house, and fallowed him down the hall, and into Edith's bedroom. He made his way across to the attached bathroom, grabbed Edith's hair brush and walked out. Xander then made his way back to the stairs and into the basement. When they reached the basement Xander walked up to the door the pretend Edith had been trying to pry open.

"But it won't open" Eddy said when Xander reached for the door knob.

"It will open" Xander said, as he turned the knob and the door effortlessly swung open. Almost instantly there was a ear splitting shriek, fallowed by a sharp searing pain in Eddy's left cheek. Before he could even respond to the pain he found him self suddenly flung backwards and landing hared halfway across the room.

"Oh I am so sorry Eddy. I didn't know it was you" said a familiar voice.

When Eddy looked up he saw a very familiar small woman with lady bug wings. Eddy smiled. It was Sara.

"It's ok" Eddy told her, not being able to stop smiling despite the pain as he plucked her needle sized sword from his cheek and handed it back to her. "To be honest I am just glad to see you are ok."

Sara smiled "I am sorry. I thought you were that changeling, but your not. I can tell. You smell like you. It smells . . . like oil" she said with a small shudder at the end.

"What happened here? Where is Edith?" Eddy asked her before she could begin to ramble.

"Well when I got here I could tell it was not Edith. It smelled all greasy and oily. Edith dose not smell oily. She smells pretty. Like sunflowers and fresh dirt. nothing like oil at all" she told them.

"Where is my sister?" Xander asked. "Do you know what happened to Edith?"

"I wish I knew" Sara said sadly. "I tried to figure it out, but the changeling caught on to me pretty quick. They tried to hit me with a fly swatter! A fly swatter!" Sara fumed.

"Sara. Sara, focus" Eddy said. "Did you manage to learn anything?"

"No, scatter brain. I already told you they came after me with a fly swatter. I remembered there was a charm on this room. So I hid in here."

"You can detect the charm?" Xander asked surprised.

"Of course I can" Sara said proudly.

"What charm?" Eddy asked as he looked at the door.

"Edith did it. Keeps anyone with ill intent from entering. It's why our changeling friend could not open the door. Now come on" Xander said as he walked through the doorway "I have a sister to find."

Sara landed on top of Eddy's head as he fallowed Xander into the room. The brightly lit room's walls were lined with cabinets covered with little four inch drawers, all neatly labeled right below their tiny brass handles. Resting in the center of the room sat a large work table made of oak.

The table had an adjustable lamp attached to one corner, and in the center a pair of magnifying glasses resting on the edge of a rubber mat along with a small pair of needle nose pliers, and a neatly organized set of what looked like dentist tools. Resting in the center of the mat was a set of silver interlocking links set with several facets and a set of gem stones resting beside them.

Xander walked up to the work table and carefully picked up the objects and set them aside. "Looks like who ever took her showed up while she was in the middle of a project."

"What is all this?" Eddy asked as he started walking around the room.

"Edith's work shop" Xander told him as he begun to pull out a series of road maps out from under the work table along with a long clear quartz crystal hanging from a silver chain. Xander began wrapping the chain around the handle of the hair brush, and Eddy came to stand next to him. "Edith is a charmer, and I don't mean as in that she is charming. She makes charms. Crafts spells. She is really quite good at what she dose. Probably the reason why someone snagged her."

Eddy looked down at the floor. "Actual, I think they took her because of me."

"Because of the statue?" Xander asked. "But how would they know you would bring it here? Besides, Sara said she was already gone when she got here. That means they took her before you ever even had the thing."

"I think they knew I would get a hold of it eventual, and then bring it here" Eddy said.

"Don't you think you are being more then a little paranoid?" Xander asked him.

"Think about it Xander. They did not just take her, they left someone behind to impersonate her. They wanted us to think she was still here. Why?" Eddy pointed out.

"Who is they, any ways?" Xander asked with out ever taking his eyes off of the crystal, as he stared at it dangling over one of the maps, twirling it slightly.

"The UnSeelie Court" Eddy told him.

Xander's face went white as he sat the brush and crystal down on the table. "What?" he exhaled.

"The UnSeelie-"

"But they don't exist any more" Xander said, cutting Eddy off.

"Apparently they do" Eddy told him.

Xander picked back up Edith's hair brush and went back to dangling the crystal over the map. "You left that part out before."

Suddenly the crystal stopped spinning on its chain and went ridged as it jabbed into the map with a slight thud, sounding like a dart in a dart board. Xander leaned in close to the map and fallowed its grid lines to the edges in order to check the coordinates. He quickly set the brush and crystal aside, and began leafing through the other maps. He pulled one out of the stack that was a more detailed version of the area the crystal had hit, and then quickly placed it on top of the other map.

"What are you doing?" Eddy asked, as Xander once again picked up the brush and the crystal.

"Finding Edith" Xander said as he began to spin the crystal over the new map. Xander took a deep breath and sighed. "It's called scrying. Using her brush and the crystal, we should be able to find her. The brush belongs to her, and so dose the hair in the brush. Combine them with the crystal on the chain, and they act like the magnet in a compass. The crystal is the needle, and Edith is north. Understand?" Eddy nodded. Then suddenly the crystal stuck to the map again. Xander checked the coordinates, pulled out another more detailed map, and began the process over again.

"So you can pin point where she is with those?" Eddy asked.

"Sadly, no. But I can get us really close. Within a few miles. But that will be more then close enough" Xander told him. "I have a tracking charm that will take us the rest of the way."

"That is great" Eddy said smiling.

Xander smiled too "you know what the best part is?" Xander asked him. Eddy shook his head. "The fact that this is working, means Edith is still alive." The crystal struck the map again. This time instead of grabbing another map, Xander grabbed a pencil instead. He then circled the place on the map where the crystal had been. "Found her!" he said as he grabbed the map off of the table and quickly sprinted out of the room.

"Well you heard the man" Sara said from atop Eddy's head. "Lets go get her back." At that Eddy quickly ran out of the room after Xander.

Chapter 18

The Castle

Xander and Eddy found themselves racing down several winding mountain roads. "Xander slow down!" Eddy yelled. "You are going to fast for me to see the street names." He then mumbled "You are also going to get us killed."

"Sorry" Xander said as he let up a little on the gas pedal. "It's just that I . . ."

Eddy placed a hand on his friends narrow shoulder. "It's ok Xander. We will find her." Xander nodded solemnly. "There! Xander turn there!" Eddy yelled, as he pointed at the right side of the windshield. Xander turned sharply and slammed his foot down hard on the brakes as tried to slow down, causing his tires to screech and leaving dark black skid marks across the surface of the road as they filled the air with the smell of burnt rubber and smoke.

Xander's little car fishtailed, and the 2X4 that he used for a back bumper broke loose and smashed noisily into the near by rock face. Despite the turn having scared the daylights out of him, Eddy managed to laugh halfheartedly as he looked behind them through the back window. "You know, I have always joked about your car coming apart on the road, but I never expected it to actually happen."

Xander laughed a little as well. "To be honest I have always thought it was just a matter of time." Now both men begun to laugh, for real this time. It felt good to laugh. Edith had always thought it would be Xander that would pay the price for Eddy's meddling in the world of magic, but it had turned out to be her, and the thought made Eddy feel sick. "Go ahead and open the glove box" Xander said. "We should be close enough for the tracking charm to work now."

Eddy opened the glove box and grabbed the glass petri dish that was resting in it and held it lightly in his hands. Xander had wrapped a piece of Edith's hair around a small piece of amethyst crystal that had a clear tip on one end, and then placed it in the dish that he had then proceeded to crudely tape shut before they had left the house.

Eddy stared down at the dish as he tipped it back and forth in his hands, causing the small purple crystal to slide around inside. "So how is this supposed to work any ways. Um . . . never mind." The small crystal in the dish suddenly slide to the center, and stayed there, as if it was glued in place. As Eddy turned the dish the crystal inside would rotate, behaving just like the needle of a compass. "So what end am I supposed to fallow?"

"The clear end" Xander told him with out ever taking his eyes off of the narrow dirt road that was now in front of him.

They passed several drives, but the crystal stayed relatively straight, shifting only as the road would twist and turn. Finally the crystal began to pull to the right. "Xander it's moving. The drive should be coming up soon." Suddenly the crystal spun to point behind them. "We passed it. Blast! Some how we passed it."

Xander slammed on the brakes, and the car skidded noisily on the gravel, dirt and ice. Before the car could even come to a full stop, he slammed the car into reverse, and backed down the road.

"There. Between those bushes!" Eddy shouted.

"I see it" Xander said as he took a hard turn down the narrow drive and began to fallow it up the mountain.

As they made their way though the dense woods they began to see a large structure through the trees. As they drew closer the building continued to grow larger and larger. "What is that?" Eddy asked as he peered through the cars side window as they approached the massive stone building.

"It . . . looks like a castle" Xander said as he came to a stop in front of the regal structure.

The four story castle rose up out of the side of the mountain, and was constructed from large stone blocks of granite. The sun gleamed off of the frosted grass and random piles of snow as they made their way down the cobble stone pathway that lead up to the buildings overzealous doors. Eddy's confidence began to waver as he gazed up at the various turrets that adorned the front of the building.

"What is a castle doing in the mountains of Colorado?" Eddy asked Xander.

"There are actually quite a few castles in Colorado. Many date back to the early days of Denver. There is one only a few blocks from your house. Not this big of course, but it is still there. Didn't you know that?" Xander asked. Eddy just shook his head. They came to stand in front of a set of beautifully carved oak doors. "Besides haven't you always wanted to storm a castle."

"I don't think the two of us can storm much of anything" Eddy said.

"So you are the cop, what is the proper procedure for this sort of thing" Xander asked him.

"We can always try knocking" Eddy said.

"Your kidding?" said Xander in disbelief.

Eddy shrugged and walked up to the door and pounded his fist a few times on the frigid surface of the wooden door resulting in a low thudding sound. After a few minutes of no one answering he tried again. Still no one answered.

"Now what?" Xander asked him.

Eddy looked at his worried friend. "You are certain she is in there?" he asked.

"Absolutely" Xander asserted with a sharp nod.

"Stand back then" Eddy said as he drew his gun and took a few steps back a couple of feet from the door himself. Eddy fired a shot at the doors lock, but the bullet just ricocheted off the metal, and bounce off into the woods with a sharp ping. He put the gun away and began to walk along the outer wall of the castle. "I guess we will try a window."

As the two made their way around the building they found several windows, but none were placed at a height that would allow anything close to reasonable access to climb through without the aid of a ladder. As they walked along the wall the slope of the mountain dropped, placing each window higher and higher until they gave way to a series of enormous stone patios. Sadly the high patios seemed to lack any visible staircases that would allow them access.

They fallowed along the exterior of the castle until they came to a small stone structure attached to the side of the main building. The near by creek had been diverted to run up along the side of the building were it proceeded to spin and old water wheel. The duo had to fallow the man made stream for a short distance before they came upon a small old foot bridge that allowed them to cross. They quickly made their way back to the structure with the water wheel, and found a small wooden door. Much to there pleasant surprise the door was unlocked. They cautiously opened it, felling it was to good to be true. Sadly it was. When they peered inside they found that the room granted no access to the rest of the house. Large gears turned inside, but no additional doors could be found. The only thing leading in, was a small pipe passing through the wall. The two men left defeated and continued on their search around the outside wall of the building.

Eventually they reached the back of the immaculate home only to find it connecting with a sheer cliff. Defeated and disappointed, the pair made their way silently back to the front yard.

"Now what?" Xander asked as they once again stood in front of the solid doors.

"Can you move the stone around them? The doors that is" Eddy asked him.

Xander stared at the door for a moment before shaking his head. "No. There cemented in place."

Eddy pounded on the door again. "Open up! This is the police!" he yelled. He picked up a loose rock from the yard, and then threw it at the door as hard as he could out of frustration. The rock bounced harmlessly off of the door and rolled across the ground.

"Now that is an idea" Xander said with a smile.

"Don't patronize me" Eddy said.

"I'm not" said Xander, as he pulled a popsicle stick out of his jacket pocket and it suddenly expanded into a long staff.

"I don't think prying it open is going to work" Eddy told him.

"Neither do I" Xander said as bits of gravel and sand began to roll across the frosted ground and climbed up his body. The earthy particles wound up his legs, and wrapped around his torso, until they finally ran down his arms and up to the highest end of the staff, transforming it into a massive mallet. Xander swung the mallet at the door with astounding force, producing no damage, just a loud echoing thud. "Sharper. It needs to be sharper" he mumbled. The material flatland, and rounded at the edges to form a large battle ax. Xander once again swung the weapon viciously, only to have the stone blade bounce off of the sturdy wood.

"Bigger. I need to go bigger." Xander transformed his staff back into a popsicle stick. At the same moment he released his control on all of the sand, gavel and little bits of rock, allowing them to drop off of his body and noisily hit the ground like little bits of petrified rain. Xander turned around and walked over to the near by rock face, and began to stare at it.

Eddy walked back up to the doors and once again began to pound on them. "Let me in!" he screamed at the doors. He pounded and pounded with frustration, and still no one answered. Finally, exhausted and defeated, he rested his head against the cold wood and weekly hit his reddened fist against the door. "Edith" he whispered, as small green sparks drifted up from his hand.

He slapped the door weakly, and more sparks rose up. If Eddy had been looking up instead of staring at the frozen ground at his feet, he would have noticed the sparks and little curls of smoke rising from his hand as the wood slowly began to darken.

"How did you do that?" Xander called out from behind him. Eddy turned to look back at Xander, and found the tall man standing near by holding a rock the size of a Volkswagen over his shoulder.

"How are you lifting that" Eddy blurted.

"Magic" Xander said simply. "But how did you burn the door?"

"What?" Eddy asked.

He turned around to find five lines of green flames crawling across the door from the ends of a hand shaped char mark. Eddy stepped back from the door, and then he looked down at his hand to discover it was wrapped in the same green fire.

"I don't know" Eddy told him.

Xander smiled "I've got an idea. Press your hand back against the door."

Eddy did as he was told, and flames quickly spread across the doors surface. Xander leaned back and then flung his arm forward, throwing the enormous rock like a pitcher throwing a ball at a baseball game. Eddy dove out of the way as the boulder crashed through the burning door, finally granting them access to the castle.

The flames on the remains of the door faded to orange as Eddy looked at his hand and watched his own flames flicker and die. Eddy hesitantly poked at his hand to see if it was hot, but was surprised to discover that it was in fact, quite cool.

Xander walked forward, paused briefly to look at Eddy's hand and patted him on the back, then he stepped through the shattered burning doors. "Good job Eddy. Now come on, let's go get my sister back."

Eddy's head snapped up, and he drew his gun as he hurried forward to take the lead. He did not know what to expect, but he knew he wanted to keep it at a distance and away from Xander. Edith would never forgive him if any thing happened to her brother.

The boulder had shredded the entry hall, leaving little burning streaks as it had passed. The earth based meteor had left nothing unscathed as it had torn through the front room, and imbedded itself in the far wall. They passed into the center of the exquisitely decorated room, unsure where to go next. Multiple doorways lead out of the room, along with a grand staircase leading up to the houses large upper levels.

There was a quick flash of motion, fallowed by the rapid pounding sound of feet as someone went running down a nearby hallway yelling "he's here. How is he here. You said he couldn't find us." Eddy thought the voice sounded familiar, but the source of the voice was to distressed for him to be certain.

"The direction of panic seems like a good place to start. Don't you think?" suggested Xander.

"Agreed" said Eddy with a nod, as the pair made their way across the room towards the hallway the panicked struck man had run down. As they made their way down the hallway they could hear a conversation coming from a room somewhere towards its far end.

"You said it was safe here" the panicked voice said.

"It is safe" said a much calmer female voice that Eddy recognized instantly as the woman from the snow storm. The woman that had killed Carl.

"It's not safe. They're here. How is that safe?" the panicked man responded. "If Vallen is with him, I am out of here. I am already down an eye thanks to her. This is not what I signed up for."

"Relax Winston. I can take care of them. I know how to handle Eddy" the woman said. Winston responded with a K9 like whine, clearly not convinced.

As they approached the closed door at the end of the hall, Eddy prepared himself to face Winston and the woman from the other night. He prepared to face what ever unknowns he would encounter as well. However nothing could have prepared him for what he found after he kicked the door open.

"Rose?" Eddy blurted out in shock as he entered the room to find his girlfriend standing behind a chair that had a heavily bruised Edith tied to it.

"Eddy what are you doing here?" Rose asked sweetly as she calmly walked towards him.

"What am I doing here? What are you doing here? Rose what is going on?" Eddy asked, unable to process what was happening. In fact, as she got closer he was finding it increasingly harder to think.

"Eddy don't let her touch you!" Edith screamed.

"You shut up!" Rose yelled back at her. When she looked back at Eddy, she was once again calm. "It's ok Eddy. Every thing is fine." She reached out and took Eddy's hand.

Every thing seemed fine. She was right. Why wouldn't everything be fine? Eddy thought. *Why am I here? Whose house is this any ways?* Eddy looked around the empty room trying to piece together how he had even gotten there, but kept coming up blank.

"Eddy" came a voice that sounded like someone screaming from faraway. It sounded familiar, but he could not remember who it was.

"Eddy. Eddy! Are you ok?" Rose asked him.

He turned around to find Rose and him standing in his apartment. She was still holding his hand. Eddy looked at her and smiled. "Yeah, I am ok. I feel like I just had the strangest dream."

"Really? What was it about?" she asked him.

Eddy thought for a moment "to be honest, I can not remember."

"Then it doesn't matter" Rose said with a smile.

Eddy shrugged "I suppose you are right."

"Of course I am right" she said as she leaned up to kiss him.

"Eddy" came the faint voice once again.

Eddy pulled back from Rose and looked around the room. "Did you hear that?" he asked her.

"Hear what? I didn't hear anything" she told him.

"Like some one calling my name" he said.

"Help" came the faint voice again.

"There it is again. Someone is calling for help." Eddy started walking towards the window and Rose pulled him back.

"I do" Rose said. Eddy turned to find her standing in front of him in a flowing white wedding gown. She smiled at him, and Eddy could not help but smile back. The minister pronounced them man and wife, and Eddy kissed his new bride. They turned to face the smiling faces of their friends and family, and as Eddy looked around the church he could not help but feel that someone was missing, someone important.

They walked their way down the aisle on there way out of the churches sanctuary. Rose never letting go of his hand. As they neared the door Eddy once again heard a faint voice screaming for help from faraway.

They stepped through the doors and Eddy suddenly found himself sitting in a chair in a hospital room. Rose was laying in a hospital bed holding Eddy's hand with one arm, and a newborn baby in the other. Eddy smiled at the two of them. "Hello there little one" he said with a smile as he looked at his newborn baby.

"Come on Edith. Say hello to your father" Rose said.

Eddy blinked and looked from the baby to Rose "What did you say?"

"I was just telling Edna to say hello."

"Help!" came a whimpered scream, sounding much closer then before.

"That is not what you called her" Eddy said as he tried to stand up, but Rose would not let go of his hand.

"Help!" came the voice again, even louder as if it was getting closer.

"Yes I did Eddy. Now sit down" Rose said, she was starting to sound irritated.

"Help" screamed the voice, now sounding as if it was right outside the door. "Eddy. Help me!"

"Who is that?" asked Eddy as he tried to walk towards the door, but could not get free from Rose's grip. He looked back at her, irritation and anger beginning to show on his face. Then be noticed there was a paned look on the baby. "What is wrong with her?"

"You are scaring Emily. That is what is wrong. Now sit down" Rose demanded.

"It's Emily now!" Eddy yelled. "Make up your mind Rose."

"It has been Elizabeth. Now sit down" Rose said as she pulled hard on his arm as she tried to get him back in the chair.

"This isn't right. What is going on?" Eddy demanded.

Suddenly the door of the hospital room flew open, and when Eddy looked at it he saw a small bruised woman tied to a chair sitting in the hall. "Edith?" he said in shock. He turned to look at Rose to ask her to explain, but when he did he found the pained look of the baby was now on Rose's face as well.

"How is this possible" she gasped. Then suddenly, Rose let go of Eddy's hand. The world bubbled, and Eddy felt like he was falling forward, and then suddenly he found himself standing back in a spacious room. Rose was standing in front of him and was now cradling a blistered hand. When he looked down at his own hands he discovered that they were wrapped in green flames. He looked from his hands to Rose, fear and panic strong on his face as he tried to understand what was going on.

Him and Rose had been in a hospital with their new baby. They had been married. Now he was suddenly in large room, Rose was hurt, he was on fire, and Edith was tied to a chair. *Edith why had I not been able to remember her? That is who's voice I had been hearing.*

"It is ok" Rose said trying to sound calm but coming across shaky as she hesitantly reached out to grab Eddy's arm.

"Don't let her touch you again!" he heard Xander yell from behind him.

Eddy turned to see Winston had fully changed into his wolf form and had one of his furry meaty arms wrapped tightly around the drows neck. "What?" he asked.

"Don't let her touch you again!" Xander managed before Winston's arm cinched up tighter around his neck, making it hard for the tall man to breath.

"Oh shut up Xander!" Rose hissed, as she firmly grabbed hold of Eddy's right arm. Suddenly, once again, Eddy found the room was empty.

"Eddy!" he heard Edith scream clearly, as if she was only a few feet away.

Rose pulled her hand back cursing, and Eddy felt himself falling forward, and once again the room had other people in it.

"YOU!" Rose spat as she turned to glare at Edith. "You are why I can't hold his mind. You are why I have been loosing control over him the last few months" she said as she began storm across the room towards Edith. As Rose's arm reached out for Edith, her nails lengthened, and thickened into claws. Her pail skin darkened to a ruddy color, and a large pair of corkscrew horns curled out of her now jet black hair. "I will kill you. Then every thing will go back" she stated. "Once you are dead, you will no longer distract him from me. Once you are dead, you won't be able to pull at his heart."

Fire leaped from the fire place and as a line of flame rapidly burned its way across the floor it changed from orange to green as it made its journey through the room. The creature that had killed Carl came to an abrupt stop as the tall wall of green flames separated her from Edith.

The demonic woman spun around to stair at Eddy, but it was no longer the beast, it once again looked like Rose. She smiled pleasantly and began to walk back towards Eddy.

"What is going on? Who are you?" Eddy demanded.

"I'm Rose" she said sweetly. "Now come on. Lets go home sweet heart."

Eddy stepped back. "No you are not. You are that thing that attacked me last night. You are the one who killed Carl. You are not my Rose!"

"Yes she is" he heard Edith call out in a choked voice. The words clearly pained her to say. "That is Rose. She is a succubus. She has been feeding on you. They ensnare your mind, and then feed on your life force."

Rose's face went stern, and then she smiled, showing a small pair of pointed fangs. "Well, now that the truth is out, I suppose there is no more need for this face" she said as her body shifted back into the demonic woman in a tank top and running shorts.

"What have you done to Rose?" Eddy asked the woman.

"As Edith said. I am Rose" she said with a wicked smile.

"You are one of them?" Eddy asked in disbelief.

"Oh you are catching on" she said, still smiling.

"You are a spy? But you can't be. We have been together sense long before any of this even started" Eddy said.

"A happy little coincidences actually. The information you have shared with me has been most helpful in helping me move up. Not that you were even aware you were sharing it with me" Rose told him. She looked back at the flames raging across the floor. "Sadly, as helpful as you have been, and as filling of a meal, I don't think I can forgive you setting my house on fire. I think this will be our final meal together Eddy." She looked back at Edith. "And killing you will get rid of these flames, and then I'll take care of her."

"Hey" Winston said from the forgotten corner of the room where he still stood restraining Xander. "I didn't sign up for killing anyone. I am no murderer."

"Shut up you sniveling pup, or you will be next. You are UnSeelie now. When you signed up with us, you signed up for a lot" Rose snarled before turning her attention back towards Eddy.

Eddy looked at Xander, and then looked back over at Edith sitting behind the wall of flame. As his gaze moved to Rose, his eyes narrowed. He now knew she had been using him. For over a year, she had seen him as nothing more then food. His love for her had been an illusion, and her love for him had been a lie. He knew that now. He bent down, and picked up the antique butter knife off of the floor where at some point it had fallen from his pocket, and he then promptly changed it into his sword. Instantly the blade was wrapped in its usual amber flame.

Rose had said Edith had broken her hold on him. As he thought about Edith his flame changed from orange to white, as the colors of his own internal flame intermingled with the sword's. As the color of the flame changed, it finally dawned on Eddy why his powers worked when they did. He looked over at Edith and smiled. It was because of her.

"What are you smiling about?" Rose asked him.

"This!" Eddy said as the wall of fire raced across the room like a glowing green wave and washed over both him and Rose.

Rose screamed in pain as the fire poured over her. As the flames subsided she laid burnt on the floor before an unsinged Eddy. She looked up at him and hissed. "You will pay for this Eddy." Wings grew from her back as she sprang up, and sprinted across the room. She ran towards the wall and then flung herself through a near by window.

Eddy ran to the window just in time to see Rose's wings carrying her off into the pine trees, and disappear. Eddy turned to see Xander standing behind him, with no sign of Winston.

"Where is," Eddy began, but was cut short.

"Wolf boy bolted when the wave of fire started" Xander told him. "I nearly did myself, to tell you the truth. That was pretty intense."

Eddy turned his attention to Edith. He walked over to the wall of fire. He paused briefly before it, and then he reached out his arm and placed his hand in the raging flames. He felt nothing. To him the flames felt cool. He then stepped through the fire, and walked up to Edith. He untied her from the chair. He then picked her up, and cradling her small battered body he carried her back through the fire, and right out of the burning mansion.

"How did you do that?" she finally asked him weakly, as he set her safely down next to Xander's car.

Eddy blushed a little. "I'll tell you another time" is all he said.

Chapter 19

The Seelie Guard

The lights lining the road illuminated the empty street harshly through the heavy rain as Edith made her way down the sidewalk. The lights reflected in the rapidly accumulating puddles like ever growing pools of gold. The large frigid rain drops stung her skin as the freezing cold water hit her face. The moister froze her to the bone as it soaked straight through her clothes. She hunched over, and pulled up her coat as she tried to shield her face. She was wishing she had brought an umbrella, or worn a rain coat, but the early winter weather was hard to predict, and the storm had surprised her, turning from light snow to poring rain in an instant. Finally she stopped in front of a old red brick apartment building. She dared a look up and the drenching rain poured across her face as she stared at the second story window, just as a dim light came on.

*　　*　　*

Eddy sat on the couch in his living room. The apartment was dark, only lit by the dim light trickling in through the rain soaked window. Eddy stared at the freezing water as it taped noisily against the windowpane. He sighed before he leaned over and turned on a small lamp resting on a nearby end table. He then proceeded to stair down at the small black box that was resting in his hands as he rested them between his knees.

Eddy creased his brow, and frowned as he flipped open the little box and looked at what was nestled inside. The light shone dimly on the small diamond resting in the top of the slender gold band. The ring was not much, but it was what he had been able to afford. At the time he bought it he wished he had been able to afford more, but now he was left wishing he had never even laid eyes on it in the first place, let alone purchased it. The ring had been meant to represent love, but now all it stood for was a lie, and that knowledge was ripping him apart inside.

He stared at the ring and tried to decide what he should do with it, when there suddenly came a knocking at the door. Eddy shoved the box in between the couch cushions as he slowly got up to see who was at the door. He opened the door ready to tell who ever it was to go away, but stopped himself when he discovered that it was Edith. She stood in his doorway shivering, her clothing sopping wet. She smiled weekly at him as she wiped several dripping strands of hair out of her face.

"How are you?" she asked as Eddy moved aside, and invited her in.

"I'm good" he said solemnly. Edith pulled off her soaked gloves and stared at him. "OK. I lied. I am not fine. What do you expect me to say. I found out today that the woman that I thought I was in love with was in fact controlling my emotionless and using me, using me . . . as food. Do you have any idea how much that hurts?"

"Yes. A little. I don't know what it's like to be someones food. But I do know what it's like to to be so hurt that it feels like you are going to break. You where not the only one who was hurt today Eddy" she told him, as she reached out and took his hand in hers.

Her hand was icy cold from the freezing rain but it felt good in his, and he smiled, if only briefly. "I know they hurt you. And I fell terrible about it. But I meant-"

"But you meant, they hurt you on the inside. So did I" Edith told him. "Some one I care a great deal for was hurt more then anyone ever should be. It is a horrible sickening feeling, not knowing what you can do to make the pain go away. Not knowing how to help them. So yes, I do know what it is like to be broken."

Eddy stared at her. "Who was it?" he asked her somberly.

"You, Eddy" she told him with a faint smile. "If there is any thing I can ever do, don't hesitate to let me know." With that she hugged him, then quickly pulled back. "Sorry. I'm soaked, and I just got you all wet."

Eddy smiled, and drew her back in. "It's ok. I don't mind" and then he hugged her tight. Eddy stood there for a long time and held his friend. It did not make the pain go away, but it did make it feel just a little bit more distant. "You had asked me how I was able to control the fire earlier today."

Edith leaned back and looked at him. "I take it you faunally found the emotion that you needed to call on your power. So what was it."

Eddy smiled at her and blushed a little as he opened his mouth to speak, then suddenly there came a knock at the door. Eddy sighed and let go of Edith. He walked over and opened the door. Much to his surprise he found the CDMA officer from the night of the raid standing on the other side. The same man who had been knocked through the window.

"Scot what are you doing here?" Eddy asked him feeling more then a little confused.

"The Seelie Court sent me for you" the man said as he looked around Eddy at Edith. "Is that Edith Moon with you?" Eddy nodded. "Good. I am supposed to bring her to. Her brother Xander is already in my car waiting for you."

Eddy looked back at Edith, who shrugged as she made her way over to come and stand next to Eddy at the door. "What is going on" Edith asked him.

"I am afraid I don't entirely know mam" Scot told them. "They just told me to come and get all of you, and that it was urgent. They thought it would help to have a familiar face come and get you Eddy, given the week you have had and all."

* * *

Eddy, Xander and Edith found themselves standing in the courtroom of the Seelie Court, all of its members were seated behind their bench and stared silently at them.

All the members of the court looked at Douglas, who took that as his cue to finally brake the silence. "Before we begin, I would like to make one thing very clear. I am against the proceedings of the court this evening, and do not agree with what is about to transpire."

"That being said" Max continued "I think we should begin. The events of the last few days have brought certain thing to light. A great threat has been revealed. A threat whose motives are still not yet known. We do know however, that they are willing to go to extreme measures to obtain them. Measures that include kidnapping, and torture, and even the brutal murder of one of our own. The murder of Detective Carl Strom. Detective Eddy Shade, Xander and Edith Moon, your involvement in these events can not be ignored.

Eddy began to try and object, but Max held up a hand to silence him, and he complied. "As a result, we are left with no other option, but to do something we have not done in nearly half a millennium. If the three of you will please stand, and approach the bench. Detective Shade, Ms and

Mr Moon, we are left with no other recourse, but to deputize you, as full members of the Seelie Guard."

"Excuse me?" Eddy said as Edith and Xander looked at each other in shock. "The what?"

"The Seelie Guard, are charged specificity with the task of keeping the UnSeelie Court in check. This threat is beyond us, and you three have proven yourselves able, not to mention that you are all three deeply involved rather you want to be or not. At the moment you three are the only active members of the guard, the first in more years then I wish to count. Feel free to recruit more. Grow your ranks. Find others you can trust. Uncover the truth, and above all else, prepare. Things will get much wost, before they get better. I have no doubt that a storm is coming, and when that storm arrives, we must be ready to fight back.

Eddy Shade
and
The City in the Lake

Chapter 1

Clash With a Titan

A tall woman picked her way through the forest. She gingerly stepped over the slushy patches of snow that littered the damp path that she followed as the creek bubbled noisily alongside her. The night was dark, but the moon was bright, and it reflected off of her silvery hair as it bounced around the blue skin of her face.

Finally the woman emerged into a small clearing that was spotted with damp picnic tables. She grinned as she approached the enormous willow that sat in the clearings center. "Oh Thena. Come out and play" the woman called to the tree. The enormous tree with its bud covered branches sat silently, as the woman stared at it. "Oh do come out. It is spring. Time for all good little dryads to wake up. And that goes even for those pretending to be them." The woman watched the tree and waited for a response. When after several moments nothing happened, she began to get mad. "Oh come out you old bat, or I will make you come out." The blue skinned woman held up her hand which proceeded to promptly burst into flames.

Suddenly two long damp roots burst from the ground and sprayed the woman with mud as they suddenly wrapped themselves firmly around her wrists. "What do you want?" came a voice from inside the tree, as two glowing emerald green eyes appeared on one of the trees many octopus like branches.

"Is that any way to greet a guest Thena?" The woman asked.

"Guest do not normally threaten to set me on fire" Thena pointed out to the woman.

"You were not answering your door. I was only going to knock. Do not go acting all snippy with me, when you are the one being rude by not answering" The blue elf looked at the gleaming wet roots and then down at her mud splattered dress. "Well this just simply will not do" she said. The wind swirled around her as the woman dissolved, and then reappeared again just a few feet farther back, her dress now sparkling clean. She rubbed her wrists and smiled. "Well that is better."

Thena stepped out from the inside of the branch of the tree, and glared at her "What do you want?"

"Just to talk" the woman said. "My name is Cecelia Ballard."

"I know who you are" Thena said curtly. "You are the blue elf that is running the UnSeelie Court." Cecelia smiled and bowed. "What do you want here?"

"I told you" said Cecelia, still smiling "to talk. I think we can benefit each other."

"I doubt that" Thena said.

"Now hear me out oh great titan" Cecelia said. "This world of ours has a terrible problem, and I have the means to fix it. It will take time, but I am well on my way to correcting things." Thena stared at the blue elf impatiently, only half listing. "With your help we can greatly accelerate our progress."

"And what is this problem?" Thena asked halfheartedly.

"Ignorance" Cecelia said with a smile.

Thena laughed "Ignorance? I am afraid that for most there seems to be no cure for that aliment."

"For some forms of it yes, but not for all." Cecelia went on "I refer to an ignorance caused by a great plight. One that infects so many humans. One you, are personally responsible for." Thena's face was now starting to show anger instead of boredom. "I am referring to the veil" Cecelia finished.

"You can not destroy the veil" Thena said angrily.

"Ah, but I can." Cecelia said proudly. "My colleges are gathering the necessary tools as we speak."

"That is not what I meant. I know it is possible. What I meant, is that it should not be done. You risk killing us all. We put the veil in place for a reason."

"Yes. To rob my kind of our rightful place" Cecelia accused.

"No, to prevent genocide" Thena shot back. "You are young-"

"I am centuries old!" Cecelia yelled, cutting her off "Do not speak to me like a child."

"Then don't act like one! Compared to me, you are not even an infant. I have seen your people rise from nothing, and then destroy themselves in pursuit of their own petty pleasure. Your very existence is not even a blink of an eye compared to the eons I have endured."

"My people were gods!" Cecelia screamed. "Then you and the other, so called, higher beings, stole that from us."

"We stole nothing. Your people were not god. They where thugs. Thanks to the actions of the blue elves the rest of us were hunted. The only way to survive was to hide. We knew that no forest would be deep enough, and no mountain would be tall enough to hide us forever. Not from the ever expanding world of the humans. So we decided the only place to hide was where they could not find us. Among them."

Thena turned away and began to walk back towards her tree. "I think this conversation is over. So if you don't mind, it is still early in spring, and I am still tiered. Good night."

"I know it is still early. That means you are still weak. That is why I came. You see if you wont help me, then I need to make certain that you don't help them."

"Them?" Thena asked.

"Detective Shade and the Moon siblings" Cecelia said. "I can not allow you to help them stop me."

Thena turned around and narrowed her eyes. "Is that a threat?"

"No. No threat. A promise" Cecelia said. "I fear no god, or even a titan. Every one has their weakness, and to be honest yours is rather obvious."

Cecelia thrust her arms forward and flames erupted from her hands and slammed into the enormous willow tree that stood behind Thena.

Thena's face filled with rage, and her eyes burned with an anger even hotter then the flames that burned her home. Massive amounts of water began to pour from the river, and washed over the tree in waves that were flung forward by enormous roots flailing in the water like stranded eels. The crests of the waves took on the shape of young children as they rose through the air. The children landed in the tree branches wear they stood with there hands stretched over their heads, as water contended to flow from the river. The water wound its way through the air in thick ribbons and coated the tree with a rippling upward cascade.

"You think that is how to kill me? As you said before, I am no dryad" Thena bellowed. "It will take more then burning a tree to be rid of me. It may be my tree. It may be my home, and I am rather found of it, but it is still just a tree, and I have others like it that I can reside in. You can not destroy them all. That is well beyond even your power. Now I think it is time for you to go!"

Cecelia looked at Thena smugly. "I don't care who you are. Do not presume to think you can tell me what to do. Fire is only a small sample of what I am capable of."

"I am well aware of the extent of your powers, and I give you one last chance" Thena said. "Leave, now."

Cecelia opened her mouth to talk, but then promptly closed it, and took a steep back. Behind Thena, the enormous willow tree began to shake violently. The ground at its base split as a root system that rivaled the branches above ripped their way free from the still partially frozen earth. The tree reared up and lumbered forward.

Cecelia fired a bolt of lightning at the tree as it came foreword. The bolt struck a branch and cracked it down its length, leaving scorch marks, but the tree never slowed. Two of the trees massive branches swung forward, just missing Thena on each side, and slammed hard into the ground next to the blue elf.

Cecelia raised her arms to take another shot, but the limbs slammed together, and she had to fly up into the air to avoid them. Thena jumped into the air to avoid the limbs as well, and landed safely on top of one of them. She began running down the limbs as they swiftly reached up towards the floating woman.

"You can not catch the wind" Cecelia yelled as the air began to swirl around her and she began to dissolve into it.

"I am the mother of trees. Trees are the masters of catching the wind!" Thena yelled, as the branch she was on swung forward and snatched the dissolving woman from the air. Instantly Cecelia solidified, and was promptly slammed face first into the mud. "Do not attempt to threaten me" Thena said, as she stepped off of the branch to stand next to the woman. Cecelia looked up from the mud and snarled before dissolving into the ground. Immediately a root shot out of the earth, griping the woman tightly. The root lowered her until she was eye level. "Don't you ever come back."

The root set the woman on her feet, and slithered back into the ground. Cecelia staggered a bit, and then fell into the near by creek, dissolved into it, and was gone.

*   *   *

"So Cecelia was here?" asked Eddy.

"Forget about that. Did you just say the veil, was created?" asked Edith in shock.

Xander just stood there staring at Thena, no longer sure what to make of her. He had always thought they had known each other pretty well, but after the story she had just told them, he was not so certain anymore. He had not expected her to tell him everything, but clearly there were bigger holes in what he knew about her then he had thought.

Thena found it hard to look at him as well. Every time she tried, guilt would begin to overcome her. "Yes" she told them. "The veil was crated. In essence, it is the greatest glamour spell ever cast."

"And you cast it?" Edith asked breathlessly.

"Yes, and no" Thena explained. "It took four of us to cast the spell. It was our only hope of survival. Humans had begun to actively hunt the other races."

"So you cast a spell so you could hide amongst us" Eddy said, not really directed at any one, but more of thinking out loud.

"And now the UnSeelie Court is trying to undo it" said Thena.

"Can that even be done?" Eddy asked.

"Any spell that can be made, can be unmade. Nothing in this world is permanent" Edith said.

"But how could they destroy the veil?" he asked.

"In theory they could do it if they collected enough of the right kind of charms" Thena said.

Eddy tensed "like an ugly little statue? About two inches tall, has a big eyeball for a head."

Edith stared at him. "Well that is rather specific."

"It's what Swan killed that man under the bridge for last summer" Eddy told them.

"That is an anti glamour charm. Why didn't you tell me about this?" Edith asked accusingly.

"Well at the time I found out about it we had to rescue you from a werewolf and, my ex" said Eddy.

Edith stared at the ground and shifted her feet uncomfortably. The question had brought up Rose, something none of them wanted to do.

"In theory" Thena said "if they amassed enough of them they could cast their own spell. Forcing all of the object to release their spell at the same time. If a large enough anti glamour spell was released, it could potentiality cause a large enough ripple to tear the veil. From there, the veil would simply unravel. This leaves you three, as the Seelie Guard, with two options. One, the impossible task of preventing them from amassing enough anti glamour charms and talismans to cast their spell. Or two, find the four items of power that were used to create the veil in the first place, and cast the spell again at the exact time the veil falls. If you time it right, no one will even notice."

Xander interrupted. "I Can't take this any longer. Thena, who are you?" he said, nearly bursting into tears.

Thena looked at him sympathetic. "I am still the woman you fell in love with. I have lived a vary long time Xander. Over the years I have been known by many names. Long ago I lived in Europe, Greece to be specific. While I lived there, I was known by the name Gaia."

"No" Edith blurted out as she suddenly sat on the damp earth having found her legs no longer able to support her. "You can't be. You're Gaia?" Thena nodded "The Gaia?"

"Yes" Thena said.

"Who is Gaia?" asked Eddy.

"Mother Earth herself. Gaia is a titan from Greek mythology. Queen of the titans to be specific. Mother of the Greek gods. Creator of the earth itself. Your a myth" Edith said.

Thena smiled at Edith. "That Gaia is a myth. I am simply the being that it was based off of, and to call me mother earth is a major stretch. Nor did I create the earth, and I am not the mother of any Greek gods. They were not gods, not as you would think of them anyways."

"So you are not even a dryad?" Xander said.

"I am the original dryad. The others are my children and grand children" Thena explained.

"So why do you go by Thena now?" asked Xander.

"When I left Greece and came to the Americas, I felt a new name was in order" Thena explained. "A new name to mark my new life in a new world." She then looked at Xander. "I never lied to you. Nor did I intend to hide my past from you. I have lived so long that to tell you everything would take longer then your life span my love. I did not tell you about who I used to be, because it happened so long ago, that it no longer maters."

Xander nodded, then manged a small smile. "So where do we find these objects you talked about?"

"I don't know" Thena said. "Sadly so much time has passed that I have long lost track of them. They are likely scattered across the earth."

"Well that doesn't exactly make option two sound so promising anymore" Eddy said somberly.

"Take heart my friend." Thena told him. "I said I don't know. I did not say that there was no one that did. I do know of someone who should know where they are. You see, when people say the earth is alive, it is more true then they know. It is indeed a living thing, and it has a voice. You can call him the green man, and I will tell you how to find him."